#8

JUNIOR HIGH

STARRING THE EIGHTH GRADE

JUNIOR HIGH

#8

JUNIOR HIGH

STARRING THE EIGHTH GRADE

Kate Kenyon

SCHOLASTIC INC.
New York Toronto London Auckland Sydney

ISBN 0-590-41161-6

12 11 10 9 8 7 6 5 4 3 2 1   8 9/8 0 1 2 3/9

Printed in the U.S.A.   01

First Scholastic printing, January 1988

Chapter 1

"*Grease!*" Tracy Douglas cried. "How totally rad!" Her blonde ponytail danced up and down as she squeezed Nora Ryan's arm. "Isn't it the most exciting thing you've ever seen?"

Nora, a short girl with curly hair and enormous brown eyes, gently pulled loose from Tracy's hand and peered at the poster. "Honestly, Tracy, give me a chance to read it."

"Well, hurry up!" Tracy pleaded. "Second bell is going to ring any minute." It was a sunny morning in early spring, and the main corridor of Cedar Groves Junior High was jammed with kids rushing to class.

"It just doesn't make sense," Jennifer Mann said thoughtfully. "Why would they advertise tryouts for *Grease* on *our* bulletin board? It's the upper class play, and we're only in eighth grade. It has nothing to do with us."

"It's weird," Nora agreed. "Of course, it could be a mistake," she said doubtfully.

"Mistake!" Tracy said, her voice rising. "What's wrong with you two? There's no mistake." She jumped from one foot to the other and hugged her books to her chest. "Don't you get it? The high school kids are going to let us try out for their play this year. I just know it!"

A red-haired boy on a skateboard skidded toward them just then, and Tracy had an inspiration. "Just a minute," she said, extending her arm like a traffic cop. Her outflung hand connected with the rider's shoulder, knocking him off balance, and he collided with a row of lockers.

"Hey — " he croaked, rubbing his elbow. "Do that again and I'll run over your toes!"

"Jason," Tracy said calmly, "read that poster and tell us what it means."

"You don't have to get violent!" Jason Anthony picked up his knapsack and glanced at the poster. "I've already read it," he told them. "There's another one just like it down by the water fountain." He started to get back on his skateboard, but Tracy covered his foot with hers.

"Not so fast. Then it's true?" she asked

breathlessly. "We really can try out for the play?"

Jason rolled his eyes, his freckles standing out in sharp contrast to his pale skin. "That's what the sign says," he said sarcastically. "Now, if you'll kindly remove your foot. . . ."

"Of course," Tracy said regally and stepped back. As Jason careened madly down the hall, she turned back to her friends with a dazzling smile. "There. You see?" she cried. "If a turnip-brain like Jason thinks it's true, it must be!"

Nora opened her mouth to question the strange twists and turns that *Tracy*'s brain was taking, but the second bell rang just then, cutting her off. She had to wait until lunch to talk it over with her best friend, Jen.

"I think she's obsessed," Nora whispered to Jen over lunch in the school cafeteria. They were sitting at a round table that was reserved for eighth-graders. As usual, the noise level in the green-tiled room was deafening.

"Tracy's possessed?" Jen's hazel eyes looked startled.

"No, obsessed," Nora said with a giggle. "All she talks about is being in that high school play . . . you know, the musical."

"Grease?" Jen mouthed silently. When Nora nodded, she glanced across the table where the pretty blonde was excitedly telling the plot of *Grease* to Susan Hillard and Mia Stevens.

"You see, the play is set in Rydell High," Tracy was explaining, "and there are two groups of kids, the T-Birds and the Pink Ladies. Danny Zucko, who is this fantastic hunk — John Travolta played him in the movie — is the leader of the T-Birds, and this really funny girl is the leader of the Pink Ladies. Her name is Rizzo."

She stopped to grab a bite of her cheeseburger when Mia interrupted her. "And Danny and Rizzo finally get together," Mia offered."

"No," Tracy said, nearly choking on a pickle. "I forgot to tell you about Sandy. She's the one he falls in love with." She paused to let this sink in, and she continued in a dreamy voice. "Sandy is blonde and beautiful, and she and Danny fall in love over the summer. They never expect to see each other again, and when they meet at Rydell, Danny dumps her."

"He dumps her?" Susan asked sharply. "I thought you said they were in love."

Tracy looked flustered. "I guess I left out some things," she said apologetically. "I should have mentioned that the T-Birds are this really macho group, and none of the boys will admit they like girls. So even though Danny wants to start dating Sandy again, he has to act like he hates her guts."

"Well, that certainly clears up the plot for me," Susan said tauntingly.

Tracy flushed, brushing her feathery bangs off her face. "You know I'm not any good at telling stories. I get everything all mixed up."

"I know." Susan snorted. "Remember seventh grade? You told Mrs. Gunter that Hamlet was unhappy because he thought his wife didn't love him."

"Well, I got him confused with Othello," Tracy said defensively. "Or was it King Lear?"

"Picky, picky," Mia Stevens said, carefully scraping the marshmallows out of her Jell-O mold. She tapped her half-gold half-midnight-blue fingernails on the tabletop and stared at Tracy. "So what happened then?"

"When?" Tracy said blankly. "Oh, you mean in *Grease*. Well, let's see, Danny and Sandy get together in the end, and so do Rizzo and Kenickie, and all the other couples."

"How sweet," Susan sneered. "Excuse me while I get sick."

"Who played Sandy in the movie?" Mia asked, ignoring her.

"Olivia Newton-John." Tracy paused.

"People say we look a lot alike," she added wistfully.

When no one said anything, Jen jumped in to fill the silence. "Yes, you do, come to think of it," she said brightly. "You're both, uh . . . blonde . . . and. . . ."

"And that's where the resemblance ends," Susan finished for her.

"I just know I'd be perfect playing Sandy," Tracy said, looking around the table. "It would be so fantastic to get the lead part."

"I'd take any part," Lucy Armanson said. Lucy was a slender black girl with a mop of shiny curls and dancing brown eyes. "You know what they say, there are no small parts, only small actors."

Jen nodded vigorously in agreement and glanced at Nora. She felt a little spark of excitement flare up inside her — the idea of being in the play was really getting to her! She wondered if Nora felt it, too. Since she and Nora had been best friends since kindergarten, each usually knew exactly what the other was thinking.

But this time, she was on her own. Nora was picking at her salad, her expression unreadable, and Jen turned her attention back to Tracy. Wouldn't it be wonderful if Nora and I could be in the play together? she said to herself. But she immediately wondered if she was being unrealistic.

After all, she didn't know the first thing about being in a play, and she knew she'd never be as confident as Tracy!

"Can you imagine what the competition will be like?" Nora said, as if she had been reading Jen's mind.

"Competition?" Tracy said, crestfallen.

"All the high school kids, plus everybody in the Drama Club, and maybe some of the kids in chorus," she said, ticking off the groups on her fingers. "And don't forget all the kids who've acted in their other productions. You *know* they'll have the edge over the rest of us."

"Stop it!" Tracy said plaintively. "You're making me discouraged before I even get started."

"I'm sorry." Nora looked surprised. "I guess I always look on the practical side of things."

"And you're absolutely right," Jen said warmly. "The rest of us get carried away, Nora. It's a good thing we have you to bring us back down to earth."

Upstairs, in the main corridor, Denise Hendrix was staring at the *Grease* poster with a wistful expression on her face. "Tryouts," she said under her breath. "That should be interesting. . . ."

The last time she had tried out for a play had been in Switzerland, she remembered.

A comic version of Hamlet. Of course it was comic! she thought with a smile. All the parts were played by females.

Her thoughts flew back to Lucerne. Just a year ago today, she had been attending an exclusive girl's boarding school in the Alps. Before that, she and her family had lived in a chateau outside Paris, a villa in Portofino, and a country house on the Yorkshire moors. There had been weekends on the Riviera, theater parties in London, and once they had even gone to dinner at the palace in Monaco.

Her father owned Denise Cosmetics. His business interests took him all over the world, and the family traveled with him. Denise had loved her exciting life, and when her parents decided to enroll her at Madame Lamarte's Château Remy, an exclusive private school in Switzerland, she was thrilled. She quickly made some wonderful friends, including a real princess, and life was perfect.

And then her world fell apart. With no warning, Mr. Hendrix suddenly decided that Denise and her brother Tony needed to grow up in the States, and Denise found herself in Cedar Groves. And worst of all, she was at Cedar Groves *Junior High*, which made her feel like an absolute baby. Of course it wasn't her fault that she lost some credits by moving around so much, but it was so embarrassing to be a whole year older than the rest of the kids. She thought she should be in high school with Tony, not stuck here in the eighth grade.

Why in the world had her father insisted on moving the family to such a small town? No matter how many times Denise asked herself that question, she could never come up with a satisfactory answer.

A sharp nudge between the shoulder blades nearly threw her off balance, and she gasped in surprise. She heard a raucous laugh, and saw a flash of red hair go whizzing by her.

"Sorry about that," Jason Anthony called, his voice echoing down the corridor.

Denise tightened the strap on her Gucci shoulder bag and started off down the hall. It was almost time for Mr. Mario's Italian class, and she knew she couldn't stand there mooning over the poster forever.

A soft movement behind her made her whirl around, and suddenly Mitch Pauley, superjock, and his sidekick, Tommy Ryder, appeared beside her, smiling hopefully.

Denise's blonde good looks had attracted every boy at Cedar Groves, and Mitch and Tommy had fallen in love with her on sight. Like a pair of bloodhounds, they had dogged her steps for months, hoping for a smile or a flicker of interest in those china-blue eyes.

"Are you okay?" Mitch asked, resting his hand lightly on her arm. "Someday that nerd is going to kill somebody."

"I'm fine," Denise said shortly, shrugging his hand off. Just leave me alone! she pleaded silently. She stared at Mitch Pauley's grinning face. She noticed he was wearing his football jersey, and waited for him to take the next step.

Mitch cleared his throat and shuffled his feet. She knew what was coming — he was going to ask her the same question he asked her every day.

"So, Denise," Mitch began in his best macho voice. He leaned closer, hoping she could smell the lemon after-shave he had borrowed from his older brother.

"Yes, Mitch?"

"Would-you-like-to-come-to-football-practice-today?" He was so nervous the words came out in a rush, and Tommy Ryder gave a delighted chortle. Mitch gave him two fast jabs in the arm, and Tommy yelped. "Coach is teaching us a new formation, and — "

"Thank you so much," Denise cut him off. She smiled sweetly. "But I'm busy. . . ." She deliberately left the sentence unfinished and hurried down the corridor.

"Hah!" She heard Tommy Ryder begin to laugh, and then there was the sound of a sharp whack. "Ow! What'd ya do that for!"

Denise smiled. At least she'd gotten rid of them for the moment. A few minutes later, she slid into her seat in Italian class, and flipped open her textbook. Except she wasn't really looking at it, she was thinking about that *Grease* poster. The boy in the sketch had reminded her of Jean-Paul, her boyfriend back in Switzerland. She wondered how she would do competing for a part in the show?

When the announcement crackled over the loudspeaker half an hour later, Denise gave up on verb conjugation to listen intently.

In her typing class, Tracy stopped typing immediately. They were in the middle of a speed run, and Ms. Jacobs, the typing teacher, hit her stopwatch and sighed heavily.

"*This is an announcement from the main office,*" the reed-thin voice of Mrs. Peters came over the P.A. "*May I have your complete attention?*" This was followed by several blasts of static, punctuated by a loud wail from Mia Stevens.

"Oh, no, I broke a nail," she announced to no one in particular. "Anybody have any glue?" Mia pushed her spiky orange hair out of her eyes, and leaned over to peer at her nail disconsolately. She was dressed as usual, in the latest punk fashion, sporting a tight black leather skirt and a pair of stiletto heels. She'd added a few silver streaks to her hair the night before, and one metallic clump drooped limply over her forehead.

"Shhh!" Tracy said furiously. "It might be something to do with *Grease*."

She sat in an agony of suspense until Mrs. Peters' voice filled the room again. *"Mr. Morgan is holding tryouts tomorrow for all those interested in appearing in"* — she paused and rustled a sheet of paper — *" 'Grease.' "*

"Omigosh," Tracy said under her breath. She clasped her hands together and accidentally hit the space bar on the electric typewriter. The carriage went whizzing dangerously to the right, like a runaway locomotive, but she was too excited to care. This could be the most important day of her life!

She stared at the speaker on the wall, willing it to spring to life again. Meanwhile, Jason Anthony spun around in his seat and gave a loud cackle. He leaned close to Tracy and struck a pose. "I've always wanted to be an actor. Which is my best side?" he asked, showing her both profiles.

"Shut up!" Tracy hissed.

"Tryouts" — another rustle of paper — *"will be at three sharp. That is all. Over and out."* Mrs. Peters departed in a final burst of static.

"That's it?" Tracy said, disappointed. "Tryouts are at three, that's it?"

"You wanted an engraved invitation?" Susan Hillard snapped.

"How will we know what to do?" Tracy wailed. "I've never even been to tryouts before!"

"It'll be okay, Tracy," Jen said encouragingly. "They'll probably tell us everything we need to know once we get there."

"We?" Nora looked at her questioningly. "I didn't know you were planning on trying out for the show."

"Well, I — " Jen blushed and bent her head over her typing manual. "I thought it might be fun to go . . . just to watch," she finished quickly.

Nora didn't answer, and just then Ms. Jacobs raised her stopwatch in the air and jabbed the starter like she was calling the Indy 500. Immediately thirty-two typewriters clattered, and Nora's fingers began to race over the keyboard. "Sure," Nora said to herself. "We'll just go to watch."

Chapter 2

"What do you think?" Tracy Douglas was saying eagerly to her friends a few hours later at Temptations. "Do we really have a chance of getting in the play?"

"There's always a chance," Lucy Armanson broke in. "But the lead? Get real!" She laughed and scooped up the last of her cherry vanilla delight. "I'm going for the chorus."

"Why shouldn't Tracy try for the lead?" Jen said loyally.

"Because you have to be realistic," Amy Williams argued. Amy was a friendly girl with a cap of shining brown hair that framed her pixie face. "Don't forget, the high school kids think we're babies — "

She was interrupted by a chorus of groans, and she held up her hand to finish: "So naturally, they're going to grab all the good parts themselves. If you just think

14

about it, you'll see I'm right." Waving her spoon for emphasis, she turned to Jen. "Tell me, Jen, what do you think of kids a few years younger than you . . . say, fifth-graders?"

Jen shrugged, and played with her straw. "Fifth-graders? They're okay in small doses, I guess. I baby-sit for one."

"Hah!" Amy said triumphantly. "I rest my case."

"Well, all that really matters is what Mr. Morgan thinks," Mia Stevens said firmly, looking around the table. "And he doesn't think we're babies. I heard that he needs a really big cast for the play, and he's counting on the junior high to help him out."

"Yeah, if you want to play the third spear in the fourth row from the back," Amy said glumly. "That's the kind of parts he has in mind for us."

"Gosh, I didn't know there were spears in *Grease*," Tracy said seriously. "I thought the whole thing was set in a high school."

Mia rolled her eyes, but Amy laughed indulgently. "I was joking, Tracy," she said. "I just meant we'll probably all end up playing extras in a mob scene."

"Not me," Tracy said softly. "I'm going to be Sandy." She wolfed down the rest of her chocolate ripple float and suddenly a stricken look crossed her face. "Do you think he's looking for someone thin for the part? Maybe I should skip dinner!"

"You look fine," Lucy reassured her. Suddenly she stared over Tracy's head, and said softly, "Look who just came in."

Denise Hendrix swept into a corner booth accompanied by her brother, Tony. If she noticed that every head turned to stare at her blonde beauty, she gave no sign.

"It's not fair," Tracy wailed. "She's even got a great-looking brother." She stared at Tony's finely chiseled profile. He was leaning across the table, talking intently to his sister, his eyes dark and serious.

"Yeah, they both got a double dose of gorgeous chromosomes," Mia sighed. "If only they'd learn to dress right, they'd be sensational."

Nora started to choke on her soda, trying not to laugh, and Jen thumped her on the back. Mia's idea of dressing right involved wildly spiked hair and enough leather to outfit Mad Max.

"It sure must be nice to have it all," Tracy said enviously. She nibbled on a vanilla wafer and tried not to stare at Denise's shimmering blonde hair.

At the moment, Denise felt light years away from having it all. She glanced halfheartedly at Temptations' oversized menu and put it down with a sigh. "I'll have a chocolate soda," she said without enthusiasm.

Tony looked at her sharply, and after they had ordered, asked, "What's bugging you, anyway?" When she remained silent, he pretended to gaze into a crystal ball. "Ah, I think I see it."

"Tony, I — "

He snapped his fingers. "Wait — don't spoil my concentration. Anthony the Amazing knows all." He touched his fingers to his temples. "Your problem is that . . . you failed your geometry test, you hate your lab partner, and someone put bubble gum in your locker combination again."

Denise shook her head.

"And worst of all, you don't have a date for Saturday night."

"Very funny," she said icily. "Although, as a matter of fact, you're right. I don't have a date for Saturday night." Or any other night, she added silently.

"And whose fault is that?" Tony countered. "There are a million guys who'd like to take you out. Except you act like they've all got the plague."

"Tony, are you nuts?" Denise said hotly. "Everyone who's asked me is at least a year *younger* than me!"

"So date high school guys."

"How am I going to meet them?" she said. "In the school parking lot?"

"I could invite some guys over to the house . . ." he offered.

"No!" she said. She played with a set of gold bangles on her wrist and said in a softer tone, "That would be awful . . . so humiliating."

The waitress appeared just then, and they were silent as she placed their orders in front of them. Tony munched thoughtfully on his cheeseburger, then said excitedly, "Wait — I've got it."

"Anthony the Amazing has had a vision?" Denise asked.

"Anthony the Amazing has a solution to your problem," he said. "The whole secret, Denise, is to meet high school guys on their own terms." He paused to let it sink in, and when her expression didn't change, he said, "Don't you get it? The play we're doing — *Grease*. Didn't I hear that it was open to the junior high kids?"

Denise shrugged. "Sure. They've got posters all over school. They're having try-outs tomorrow."

"That's it, then. All you have to do is be there." He paused. "You *are* planning on going, aren't you?"

"I — well, I hadn't really planned on it," she hedged.

"Denise," he pleaded. "You're nuts if you don't go. You can get any part you want in that thing, and you know it. And once you're in the play, you'll be around kids your own age. You'll feel a hundred percent better, believe me."

Denise fingered a strand of her golden hair. "I guess I could give it a try, just to see what would happen."

"I *know* what will happen," Tony said. "My sister will walk off with the lead."

"C'mon. . . ." Denise bent her head over her chocolate soda, secretly flattered at Tony's confidence in her. "It's been a while since I auditioned for anything."

"It will all come back to you, Denise. In a flash," he promised. "Remember," he said, popping a dill pickle in his mouth. "Go for the lead."

"I've never seen Tracy so enthusiastic about anything before," Jen said later, sitting cross-legged on her pink comforter. It was nearly six o'clock, and the sounds of *The Flintstones* reruns blasted from her brother Eric's room next door.

"You mean about anything that isn't wearing an argyle sweater and a Swatch," Nora said wryly.

"That's true," Jen giggled. She bent her head over her knees and started brushing her long black hair. "You know, getting a part in the play might be the best thing that could happen to her. She won't have time to think about boys twenty-four hours a day."

"Hmmm, I wonder," Nora said doubtfully. "Of course, it could have just the opposite effect."

"What?" Jen said in a muffled voice.

"I said ... never mind," she murmured. She smiled at Jen's upside-down head. Jen's so kind, she thought. She always wants to think the best of everyone. "You may be right," Nora said agreeably. She shrugged into her red jacket and picked up her books. "Well, I better be going. . . ."

"Oh, not yet," Jen said, suddenly appearing from under a cloud of black hair. "There's something we need to talk about."

Nora stared at her and bit back a smile. "You look like someone doing a Joan Jett imitation."

"Joan Jett? Oh, you mean the hair," Jen said, craning her neck to see herself in the mirror over her dresser. She quickly brushed her hair back and clipped the sides firmly with imitation tortoiseshell barrettes. "There — that's better. Okay," she said brightly, jumping off the bed. "Now, how will we handle tryouts? Should we go for the chorus or try for speaking parts?"

"I can't believe it — you're really serious about this?" Nora said, surprised. She slowly unzipped her jacket and dropped into a chair.

"Well, of course I am!" Jen said. She flipped on the radio and she did a little dance step as Phil Collins' voice flooded the room. "I really want to be in *Grease*. Don't you?"

"As what?"

"I don't know," Jen said vaguely. "As a singer, or dancer, or maybe just a bit part. You know, the kind where you just walk across the stage and have a couple of lines."

"Well, it's a relief to know you're not trying out for the lead," Nora said teasingly.

"Oh, I'd never do that." Jen's hazel eyes were serious. "Tracy wants it more than anything in the world." She paused, and then said, "Why are you looking at me that way?"

Nora shrugged. "I guess I'm a little puzzled. Sometimes I can't quite figure you out."

"Well, that shouldn't be too hard. We've been best friends since kindergarten," Jen reminded her.

"I know," Nora said slowly. "So how come you've never shown any interest in being on the stage before?"

"That's not true!" Jen said, pirouetting on one foot. "I played a pumpkin in the Thanksgiving pageant in third grade. You should remember that, Nora," she added reproachfully. "We were in the show together. You were a gourd."

"I was *not* a gourd," Nora said stiffly.

"You were, too!"

"It was more like a summer squash," Nora said, breaking into a grin. "Do you remember when you sat in that rocking chair? Your pumpkin costume was so bottom heavy, you couldn't get up!"

"I remember," Jen said ruefully. "I had to say all my lines sitting down. A good thing the pumpkin wasn't crucial to the plot."

They were still giggling when Jeff Crawford peered around the doorway a few minutes later. "Dinner's almost ready — oh, hi, Nora!" he said cheerfully. "Want to take potluck with us? We're having Beef Encore."

"Encore?" Nora frowned. "I think we learned that word in French class."

"It means beef *again*," Jen said, rolling her eyes. "Jeff tries to give fancy names to his leftovers. He thinks he can fool us that way."

"Sometimes it works," Jeff said with a grin. "Well, should I set an extra place?"

"No, thanks, I've got to run." Nora smiled at him. "I'm making this really neat vegetarian dish for dinner — it's got bulgur and tomatoes in it."

Jen groaned. "Some choice!"

Jeff laughed. "You just don't realize what a great chef I am," he said, heading down the hall.

"I sure know what a great *guy* he is," Jen said, when he was out of sight.

Nora nodded seriously. Jen's mother had died when she was young, and Jeff Crawford, a stocky man in his early fifties, had joined the family soon afterward as a housekeeper. He had helped raise Jen and Eric, and was one of the most important people in their lives.

"Sure you can't stay?" Jen said hopefully. "I really need your advice about tomorrow, you know."

"Don't worry, I'll call you later," Nora said. "After I tackle my homework, okay?"

"Deal!"

"I've heard about eating on the run, but this is ridiculous," Nora's mother said an hour later.

"I know, but I've got tons of stuff to do tonight," Nora told her. She was standing over the kitchen sink, scraping the remaining tomatoes off her plate.

"Really? What's up?"

"Well, I've got a biology midterm coming up," Nora said, rinsing her dish in the sink, "plus a French quiz and a history paper."

"You do sound swamped," her mother said sympathetically. "We'll have the house to ourselves tonight," she added, "and it's just as well, because I brought home a lot of work from the office." She was sitting at the round oak table, flipping through some legal briefs. "Your father's meeting probably won't break up till ten, and Sally's at a dance audition — "

"The audition! I knew there was something else I had to do!"

"You're going to your sister's dance audition?"

"Hardly!" Nora said with a laugh. "Jen is bound and determined to audition for a school play tomorrow, and I promised to give her a ring and talk about it." She poured a glass of milk and said thoughtfully, "What I'd like to do is talk her *out* of it."

"Honey, why? I think it would be good for Jen. You know how shy and quiet she is. Sometimes being onstage brings people out of their shell."

"I think Jen is fine just the way she is," Nora said firmly.

When the phone rang at eight o'clock, Nora knew who was calling. She and Jen had a nightly ritual of checking in with each other when they were finished doing their homework.

"Nora!" Jen's voice raced over the wire. "I just couldn't wait another *minute* to talk to you. Have you been working on an audition piece?"

"An audition piece?" Nora said, puzzled.

"Aren't you going to memorize something to recite for Mr. Morgan tomorrow? You're not just going to go in there empty-handed, are you?"

"Actually, that's exactly what I was going to do," Nora muttered. She started penciling in the answers to the chapter review in her French book. At the rate she was going, she'd be up half the night.

"Nora! I think you should prepare something — "

"Look, Jen," Nora said wearily, "I've thought about this, and I've just about made up my mind not to go through with it."

"Nora!" Jen pleaded. "I need you there tomorrow." She paused. "And I want you to try out with me. It won't be any fun being in the show without you."

"Jen, I just don't know," Nora began. "You know how important my grades are to me. I want to get into medical school more than anything in the world."

"You'll still have time to study, I promise! We'll just try out for small parts. That way, we won't have to spend much time in rehearsals." There was a long moment of silence, and then she said in a small voice, "Please, Nora. I'm really counting on you."

With a deep sigh, Nora closed her French book. After all, this was what friendship was all about, wasn't it — being there when someone needed you? "Okay, Jen, you win." As soon as the words were out, she was rewarded with an earsplitting shout of gratitude.

"Oh, I knew I could count on you, Nora. I just knew it!"

"I'm glad you're happy," Nora said. She tucked the covers up around her neck and cradled the phone on the pillow. "Now tell me," she said, reaching for a pencil. "What's all this about an audition piece?"

Chapter 3

"I feel as if someone tied a knot in my stomach," Jen whispered to Nora the following afternoon. It was three o'clock, and they were sitting side by side in the high school auditorium, waiting for *Grease* tryouts to begin.

"I know!" Tracy Douglas was sitting directly in front of them, and she turned around to give Jen a sympathetic smile. "I was so nervous I couldn't sleep last night." She paused and whisked out her compact. "It's a good thing we had a lab today. I can always doze off because I sit in the back."

"Amazing," Susan Hillard muttered to no one in particular. "The girl has the brain of an anteater." Susan was sitting at the end of the row, slumped low in her seat, pretending to read the latest issue of *Seventeen*.

Nora scanned the crowded auditorium and was surprised at how many junior high kids had turned up. She recognized a halo of spiky orange hair in the front row — Mia Stevens — and she saw Mitch Pauley and Tommy Ryder sitting off to one side.

"I changed my clothes three times," Tracy said nervously. "Do I look okay?" She was wearing a camouflage top over a khaki-colored T-shirt, with a pair of olive drab baggy pants.

"You look wonderful," Jen assured her. "Everything's new, isn't it?"

Tracy nodded happily. "It's the safari look."

"You look great," Susan echoed. "Perfect for hunting water buffaloes." She chortled and buried her head in her magazine.

Tracy's lower lip trembled and her wide, gentle eyes clouded over. "Why does she hate me so much?" she said in her little-girl voice.

"She doesn't hate you," Jen said quickly. "She's probably just as nervous as the rest of us and doesn't want to admit it. Nobody likes auditions and — "

The rest of her sentence was lost as someone crashed a baton sharply against the podium. Startled, Jen looked up to see Mr. Morgan, the high school drama teacher, glaring at the audience. He was an imposing figure with piercing black eyes and a mop of unruly silver hair.

"You will come to order," he commanded in a voice that could curl toenails. A hush immediately fell over the auditorium. He waited a moment, and then said abruptly, "I am Charles Morgan, the director of this play." He consulted a heavy gold watch. "We are beginning three minutes late today. This will never happen again."

Jen shifted uncomfortably in her chair, and her notebook fell to the floor.

Whack! The baton crashed against the podium again, and Mr. Morgan bellowed, "I will have no distractions while I am talking! Is that understood?" He took a step toward the footlights and said impatiently, "Put your books, your papers — everything — under the seat. Right now!"

"Who is this guy?" Susan Hillard muttered.

"Susan, please, you'll get us in trouble," Jen said nervously. She quickly stashed her notebook out of sight, feeling her heart leapfrogging into her throat.

Luckily, Mr. Morgan didn't hear Susan or Jen, and after a moment, he returned to the microphone.

"So," he continued, "does anyone know *why* this will never happen again?" No one had the nerve to answer, and after sweeping the room with his eagle eyes, he said flatly, "Because if any of you are late, you will be automatically out of the show." He drew his hand across his throat. "Out, finished, kaput. Is that understood?"

But we're not the ones who were late — you were! Nora longed to say. But she kept her opinion to herself and turned her attention back to the stage.

"We're going to cast the major parts first," Mr. Morgan was saying, adjusting a pair of rimless spectacles on the bridge of his nose. "Then we'll do the bit parts, and finally, the chorus."

He snapped his fingers and a half dozen kids wearing yellow blazers rushed down the aisles with stacks of mimeographed sheets of paper. "This is the publicity crew for the Drama Club," he said, waving his hand at the kids, "and they will take your name and pass out sections of the script to you. Remember, major roles only."

Nora watched as Tracy reached for a sheet of dialogue marked SANDY. Her blue eyes widened as she looked over the lines, and she took out a pencil and began underlining key passages.

"I'm so glad we're not going up there first, aren't you?" Jen whispered to Nora. "I've got butterflies just sitting here watching."

Nora nodded and glanced at her watch.

From the look of things, they were going to be here for hours.

In the back of the auditorium, Denise sat nervously crossing and uncrossing her legs. What was she doing here anyway? She must have been out of her mind to listen to Tony — what did he know? She didn't *want* to be in the play. She'd wait until the tyrant onstage was looking someplace else, and then she'd make her exit.

A few minutes later, she started to get up, and froze when she saw a familiar profile and a flash of blue-black hair. It was Jean-Paul! But no, that was impossible. Jean-Paul was back in Switzerland, miles away from Cedar Groves. The boy turned then, and Denise realized that the resemblance was only an illusion — a trick of the light. This boy was remarkably good-looking, though, with high cheekbones and a fantastic smile.

And he was trying out for a major role, she noted, sitting down slowly. It would have to be the lead — with a face like that, anything else would be a waste. She took another look at the dancing black eyes, and caught herself smiling. Yes, this boy was definitely star material. All he needs, she thought impishly, is the perfect leading lady — me!

Looking at Cody Miller, Tracy Douglas

felt her confidence evaporate. Not only was he the best-looking boy she had ever seen, but he just radiated excitement. Yes, that's it, she thought. She had heard about people having star quality, but she had never experienced it personally. Now, as Cody walked diagonally across the stage toward her, she felt the full force of those dark eyes, and her knees turned to Jell-O.

"Take it from the top of page three," Mr. Morgan ordered. "Danny and Sandy have just met in the school parking lot," he added in a bored voice.

After Tracy read her line, Cody shrugged and ran his hand through his dark hair. He was dressed in a black muscle T-shirt, and black chinos, and wore a heavy ID bracelet. He had the fifties look down pat, and when he spoke, he sent shivers down her spine. He stood there grinning at her, waiting for her next line. Tracy cleared her throat nervously and began reading her answer in a quivery voice.

"I changed my plans," she said. As soon as the words were out, she felt like kicking herself. Her reading was so bad, she half-expected Mr. Morgan to crash the baton against the podium again. She sounded as if she were reading the words off the back of a cereal box! Now I'll never get the part, she thought disgustedly. She wanted to disappear into the polished floorboards.

There was a long pause while Cody looked at her. He's a wonderful actor, she thought, and you could almost see the wheels turning in his mind: Should he throw his arms around her, or should he play it cool in front of his friends? Peer pressure won out, and Cody made a sarcastic comment.

As he turned to leave, his eyes locked with hers, and something magical happened: She suddenly knew exactly how Sandy felt! A hard lump forced its way into her throat, and for just a minute, she thought she was going to cry. She looked up at Cody, and it was almost as if a surge of electricity passed between them. She was sure the rest of her lines sounded more convincing, and when the scene was over, even the director seemed to approve.

"Very interesting, Miss Douglas," Mr. Morgan said when she took her seat. "A tentative quality . . . a touch of vulnerability." He gave her a thin smile. "We shall see." He turned to Cody, who was heading for the wings. "Wait a minute, young man. I want to have a word with you. Everyone else take a five-minute break." He checked his watch and stood up. "And that means exactly what it sounds like — three hundred seconds," he said acidly.

"How was I?" Tracy said worriedly.

She was splitting a soft drink with Nora and Jen in the back of the auditorium.

"You were great," Jen said. "I can really see you playing the lead."

"You and that boy — Cody Miller — make quite a team," Nora said encouragingly.

"But do you think Mr. Morgan liked me?" She brushed a lock of blonde hair out of her eyes. "He said I was . . . tentative."

"And vulnerable," Nora added. "That means he liked you, silly. I think those are just the qualities he's looking for."

"You think so?" Tracy asked breathlessly. Her hands were still trembling from the audition.

Nora smiled reassuringly. "I know so." She glanced at her watch and made a face. "Uh-oh, we've been gone four and a half minutes. Let's get back there before Mr. Morgan breaks that baton over someone's head."

"Is anyone else trying out for Sandy?" Mr. Morgan said a few minutes later to a thin girl sitting next to him.

She adjusted her horn-rimmed glasses and consulted a clipboard. "No, Douglas was the last one."

Tracy gripped the arms of the auditorium seat so tightly, her knuckles were white. She knew she was better than any other Sandys who had auditioned. Maybe she *did* have a chance of getting the lead. Maybe —

"There's one more," a low, husky voice called out from the back of the auditorium.

Tracy swiveled in her seat and peered in the darkness. Who was it?

Suddenly Denise Hendrix appeared in the center aisle. She was walking rapidly toward the stage and looked beautiful, blonde . . . and *confident*, Tracy realized with a sinking feeling.

"But you didn't sign in," the girl with the glasses said reproachfully. She pushed the clipboard at her, but Denise waved it away as if it were an annoying insect.

"I just made up my mind," she said sweetly. She stood staring at Mr. Morgan, and Jen thought that she had never seen her look more fantastic. She was wearing a pair of white denim overalls with a black tank top, and she looked gorgeous.

Mr. Morgan looked amused. "Then go ahead," he said, with a low bow. "Your public is waiting."

Nora and Jen exchanged a look. Poor Tracy, Nora thought. Now that Denise was in the running, anything could happen.

Tracy watched in disbelief as Denise and Cody began doing the opening scene together. *Our* scene, she moaned silently. Cody made all the same moves, even sending Denise one of those sultry glances, and Tracy wanted to murder him.

She had to admit they made a striking couple; Denise's blondness matched with Cody's dark looks. And Denise was playing the scene a little differently than she had, Tracy noticed. She was struggling to put her finger on it, when Jen leaned forward and jabbed her in the shoulder.

"He wants you up there again!" Jen was saying urgently. "Hurry!"

Tracy scrambled to her feet, and the thin girl thrust a script in her hand.

"I want you to try the scene in the second act, Tracy," Mr. Morgan said. "It's the sleep-over at Rizzo's, so we'll need some other girls to cue you on your lines. Any volunteers?"

Before she even realized what was happening, Nora found herself being propelled on the stage by Jen.

"What am I doing here?" she whispered, panicky.

"You volunteered," Jen said innocently.

Once the initial shock had worn off, Nora found herself enjoying the experience of being onstage. She was told to read the part of Frenchie, and Jen was assigned to read Marty. To their surprise, Mia Stevens was reading the role of Rizzo, and she was drawing a lot of laughs from the audience.

Tracy was center stage, though, and it

was obvious that Mr. Morgan's attention was focused on her. Do I really have a chance at the lead? Tracy thought nervously. She tried to focus on the lines and blot out everything else. . . .

Chapter 4

"Well folks, today's the day," Jason Anthony said, nudging his tray against Nora's in the cafeteria line. It was two days after tryouts, and Mr. Morgan had promised to post the cast list by three o'clock that afternoon.

"I know," Jen said softly. "I don't think I can stand any more suspense." She automatically slapped Jason's hand away as he grabbed a maraschino cherry off her Jell-O whip.

"Ouch! Is that any way to treat a star?" he yelped. "Someday you'll be asking for my autograph!"

"No way," Lucy Armanson said. She bypassed the mystery meat special and reached for a tossed salad.

"Hah! That shows how little *you* know," Jason retorted. He lifted a bran muffin off Nora's tray and whizzed ahead of them toward the cashier.

"Hey — give that back!" Nora yelled after him. "It's the last one."

Jason flashed a wicked grin and crammed half the muffin into his mouth.

"Oh, forget it," Nora said, fumbling for her wallet.

"There's probably enough fiber in the meat loaf to meet the recommended daily allowance," Jen said.

Lucy hooted with laughter. "There's probably not even any meat in it. Just enough fiber to make a tree!"

"I'll have a salad, fruit, and plain yogurt," Nora said firmly.

Later, when they were all seated at the center table, Amy Williams said in a tentative voice, "What was all that about Jason being a star? You don't think he *knows* something about the casting, do you?"

"What could he know?" Nora said practically.

"There've been a lot of rumors," Susan Hillard said. "Although I can't imagine why a geek like Jason would have inside information."

"He wasn't even at the audition, was he?" Lucy asked.

"He sat right behind me," Susan replied. "And I saw him go up and talk to Mr. Morgan when tryouts were over." She gave a sharp laugh. "I'd sure love to know what *that* conversation was all about!"

"I noticed that, too," Lucy volunteered. "Jason was acting as crazy as ever, and Mr. Morgan was laughing — can you imagine? Wouldn't it be funny if — " She broke off suddenly as Tracy Douglas collapsed in a chair next to her.

"Omigosh!" Tracy gasped. "It's up. The cast list is up!" She gripped Lucy's arm as if it were a life preserver, and her blue eyes were glassy.

"Tracy, are you all right?" Nora asked. Tracy's face was unnaturally pale and her blonde hair was disheveled.

Tracy nodded. "I . . . think . . . so," she wheezed. "I ran all the way here from the auditorium."

"Well, what does it say?" Susan demanded. "Did we get parts or not?"

"I . . . I . . . ." Tracy's teeth were chattering so much she could hardly talk.

"Tracy, calm down and take a deep breath," Nora ordered.

"What's wrong with her?" Susan said, irritated. "It's sixty degrees out and she's acting like she's in Alaska."

"It's just nerves," Nora said briskly. She reached over and patted Tracy's hand. It felt like a block of ice. "Now breathe, Tracy, before you start hyperventilating!"

Tracy dutifully gulped in a mouthful of air. "You're in . . ." she said shakily to Jen. "And you, too, Nora."

"We are?" Jen shouted. She threw her arms around Nora and yelled, "I can't believe we made it!" Then she calmed down and said, "What about Lucy?"

"She and Amy are in the chorus," Tracy told them. "You and Nora are Pink Ladies. And Mia . . . Mia got the part of Rizzo."

"I can't believe it," Nora said, stunned. "We actually got speaking roles."

"What about me?" Susan Hillard asked pointedly.

"Oh," Tracy said, biting her lip. "You . . . uh . . . got a part. Except. . . ."

"Except what?"

"You're, uh, sort of an understudy. For Jen."

"What! I don't believe it!" Outraged, Susan jumped up and scraped her chair back. "There must be some mistake," she said sharply, scooping up her books. "If you got a part, anybody can," she told Jen.

"Wow, she's really mad," Lucy said quietly after Susan stormed out. She speared an olive and snapped her fingers. "Hey, aren't we forgetting something? Tracy, did you get a part?"

"That's the crazy thing," Tracy said slowly. She took a sip of Jen's iced tea, and the color started to come back to her cheeks. "Yes and no."

"Yes and no?" Jen asked, puzzled.

"Two people got chosen for call-backs

for Sandy." She paused, her blue eyes wide and serious. "Me . . . and Denise."

Denise had been staring at the cast list in the main corridor for five minutes, trying to figure out her next move. She'd never gone to call-backs before. Her drama teacher in Switzerland always made all her decisions at tryouts. It was a lot simpler that way, she decided. You were either in — or out. Never in between. What was Mr. Morgan looking for, anyway? she wondered. Had she played the scene wrong? Too sure of herself? Too hesitant? Darn it all, she needed an outside opinion on this! Someone who would be impartial and fair. . . .

"Going to your class?" A cheerful voice behind her made her jump, and she turned to see Jen's smiling face.

"I — sure," Denise said. She managed a casual smile. "I'm not ready for a pop quiz, though."

"Maybe Mr. Mario will forget all about it," Jen agreed. "Everybody's too excited over the cast list to really concentrate on sentence structures, anyway."

"It looks like you're all set for *Grease*," Denise said teasingly. She flipped Jen's long brown ponytail behind her back.

Jen laughed. "I've been wearing my hair this way since tryouts. I thought it might help me get in the spirit of the fifties." They walked down the corridor and paused at the entrance to Mr. Mario's class. "Plus, I guess I'm a little superstitious. I know it sounds silly, but I figured it might bring me luck."

"Well, it certainly did," Denise said warmly. "You're going to be one of the Pink Ladies." She paused. "I'm going to need a little luck myself, you know."

"I saw your name down for call-backs for Sandy," Jen told her. "Congratulations. You must be really excited."

"Terrified is more like it," Denise said. "I've never gone to call-backs before. I'm a nervous wreck."

Jen stared at her in surprise. Surely Denise Hendrix — the most sophisticated girl at Cedar Groves — wasn't feeling unsure of herself? "But you were fantastic at the audition," Jen told her. "What are you worried about?"

Denise shrugged. "I don't know. I guess I'm just afraid I'll blow my chance. I don't know if I should play the scene the way I did at the audition or change it . . . or what." She thought for a moment. "Jen, could I ask you a big favor?"

"Name it." Jen grinned at her.

"Could you help me practice for call-backs? All you'd have to do is cue me on the lines, and tell me what you think."

"Gosh, I — "

Out of the corner of her eye, Denise saw Mr. Mario striding toward the classroom. She'd have to settle this fast. "It would really mean a lot to me. . . ."

"I . . . well, of course," Jen blurted out. Denise looked so worried and vulnerable, Jen knew she just had to help her! "I'll be glad to," she added. "We can work on it today."

"Thanks." Denise squeezed her arm. "You're a real friend."

"You did what?" Two hours later, Nora stopped dead in her tracks and stared at Jen in amazement. The last bell had just rung, and they were stashing their books in the greenish-gray metal lockers in the main corridor.

"I told you," Jen said patiently. "Denise needed someone to help her with her lines. . . ."

"And you volunteered," Nora muttered. "Honestly, Jen, you've got to learn to say no."

"Well, I couldn't," Jen said defensively. "When I see somebody who needs help, I can't just pass them by."

"I know," Nora said in a softer voice. She sighed and slammed her locker door shut. Jen was always getting involved in causes. She loved animals and did volunteer work at the local shelter, she baked cookies for the folks at the retirement home, she even collected clothing for kids at an Indian reservation in Arizona. Nora thought it was all part of what made Jen so special. But getting involved in the battle between Tracy and Denise was a different thing altogether. . . .

"Why are you so annoyed with me?" Jen asked, her hazel eyes showing hurt.

"I just think Denise can look after herself," Nora said shortly. "And anyway, what about Tracy?"

"What about me?" a girlish voice piped up. Tracy Douglas stood smiling at both of them. She was wearing a cotton twill flight suit with a leopard print belt and had tied her blonde hair back into a sleek knot.

"We were just . . ." Jen began. She stopped and looked helplessly at Nora.

"We were just saying we hope you get the part of Sandy," Nora jumped in quickly.

"Oh, gosh! Me, too!" Tracy said feelingly. "Are you guys busy right now?" she asked anxiously. "I've got a giant favor to ask."

"I'm free," Nora offered.

"Good," Tracy said gratefully. She pushed her aviator sunglasses up on her head and tucked her books under her arm.

"Can you help me with my lines? You know, call-backs for *Grease* are tomorrow and I'm a nervous wreck!"

Nora looked at Jen steadily for a moment, then turned back to Tracy. "Sure, Tracy," she said. "*I'll* be glad to."

"How did it go?" Nora asked Jen later that evening. Nora was sitting up in bed with the phone crunched against her ear, and her French book balanced on her knees.

"It was . . . okay," Jen said cautiously. Was she imagining it, or was there really a chilly undertone in Nora's voice? She tucked a pillow behind her head and played with the cord on her princess phone. "We went over the scenes for a couple of hours at Denise's house. She's really talented, you know," she said earnestly. "She was even better than she was at tryouts."

"Well, I'm glad you think so," Nora said stiffly.

This time Jen couldn't miss the sarcastic edge to Nora's voice and she jumped in to protest. "Now wait a minute," Jen said hotly, "I'm not saying I think she should get the part, I'm just saying — "

"That you think she's great," Nora said sweetly.

Jen was silent for a moment. She and Nora were best friends. Why were they arguing over this? "How did things go with Tracy?" she asked quietly.

"Fine," Nora said briskly. "As far as I'm concerned, she *is* Sandy. I cued her on her lines, and she's got a lot more confidence." She paused. "She wondered where *you* were today. . . ."

"I told her I was busy," Jen said quickly.

"I know, but she saw you and Denise getting into her brother's car. It's a little hard to miss a BMW in the school parking lot, you know."

"I see," Jen gulped. Why did this have to happen? The last thing she wanted to do was make an enemy of Tracy! And worst of all, it looked as if she and Nora were going to be at odds over this thing.

Nora changed the subject then, and asked a question about French homework. She and Jen talked for a few more minutes, but somehow the conversation seemed strained, and a little while later, they hung up.

When Nora replaced the receiver, she pulled the quilt up under her chin, and sat that way for a long time. Funny, she thought, this is the first time that Jen and I have been on opposite sides of an issue. I guess the only thing to do is wait till callbacks. Once Tracy gets the part, everything will be okay again.

A few blocks away, Jen stared at herself in her bedroom mirror, brushing her long black hair. Nora didn't even ask me what I was wearing tomorrow, she thought sadly. She glanced down at her brand-new "I love my cat" nightshirt. Oh, well, I can tell her about it tomorrow night. By then, Denise will have the part, and the whole thing will be settled.

Chapter 5

"Are you going to watch call-backs?" Nora asked the next day. She and Jen were standing alone in the dingy hallway outside the high school auditorium. The three o'clock bell had already rung, and the building was almost deserted.

"Denise asked me to be here. I guess she wanted some moral support." Jen's hazel eyes were serious and she shifted her books nervously from one arm to the other. "How about you?"

Nora shrugged. "Same thing," she said coolly. "Tracy was a nervous wreck, but I think she'll be fantastic once she gets in there," she added, motioning to the darkened auditorium.

"Denise has been pretty calm about the whole thing," Jen said. "Of course, she's been in a lot of plays in Switzerland. She's got a great singing voice, you know, and I think she has a photographic memory."

Jen gave a soft, nervous laugh. "She's already got the lines to the first scene down pat."

"Tracy's a wonderful dancer," Nora said loyally, twisting a loose wire on her spiral notebook. "You saw how fast she picked up those steps at the audition." She paused, avoiding Jen's eyes. "Anyway, experience isn't the only thing they look for in casting. Tracy's just . . . a natural actress. She's perfect for the part."

Jen was going to reply when a soft cough made her turn around. "Wish me luck," Tracy said in an overly bright voice. She was wearing a pale blue ruffly blouse that exactly matched her eyes, and a pair of white clam-diggers.

"You'll be great," Nora said warmly. "And I love your pants — they're just like the pedal pushers the girls wore in the movie."

Tracy smiled her thanks and turned to Jen, obviously waiting for her to say something. "You look wonderful," Jen began, feeling like a traitor. Luckily she was spared having to think of something else to say, because the sharp tapping of high heels made all three girls turn in surprise.

"It's Denise," Nora said in a low voice, watching a vision in a pale pink sun dress approach them. Denise had never looked more lovely. Her full-skirted cotton dress accented her tiny waist, and her blonde hair billowed in a shimmering cloud around her shoulders. She radiated self-confidence, from her leggy stride to the haughty expression in her cornflower-blue eyes.

Jen moved forward to meet her, captivated by Denise's dazzling smile. No, she said silently, it's not Denise. It's Sandy!

A few minutes later, when Nora and Jen slipped into seats in the back of the auditorium, five blonde heads were already visible in the front row.

Five Barbie dolls, Nora thought, amused. Denise and Tracy were sitting as far apart as possible, and both kept their eyes riveted to the stage, where Mr. Morgan was having a conference with Cody Miller. In spite of all his yelling, Mr. Morgan was an excellent drama coach, Nora realized, as she watched him walk Cody through his role as Danny.

"But I just don't get it, Mr. Morgan," Cody was saying in a husky drawl. "What's Danny's motivation in this scene?" Cody had worn his black muscle T-shirt again, and it was obvious that he thought of himself as the next John Travolta. He ran his hand through his thick dark hair self-consciously and kept glancing at the girls in the front row.

Mr. Morgan rolled his eyes. "Forget what you learned about motivation, Cody," he said with heavy patience. "We're only doing a run-through today so we can audition for Sandy." He took a piece of chalk out of his pocket and made a couple of X's on the stage floor. "All I want you to do is walk up to here, react, give a line, then cross stage left, and give your next line. Got it?"

Cody shuffled uncomfortably. "Well, like, it would really help if I *felt* it, you know. . . ." His voice trailed off as he squinted into the auditorium.

"Just do what I'm asking you to do!" Mr. Morgan thundered.

Denise, waiting for her turn, rubbed her damp palms on her skirt. She was more nervous than she'd ever been in her whole life, and her stomach pitched at the thought of getting up on that enormous stage.

What's wrong with me? she thought angrily. It's only a high school play, not Broadway or London's West End. She looked at Cody staring sulkily at Mr. Morgan, and she knew what was wrong. The brooding dark eyes, the long, lanky body — it was Jean-Paul all over again. She had to get Cody's attention, she decided, and the only way to do it was to get this part!

"Take it from the top. Again," Mr. Morgan said wearily two-and-a-half hours later. Someone cranked open a window in the dimly lit auditorium, and Tracy shivered as a chilly breeze swept across her shoulders. Or maybe it was nerves, she decided. At this point, she couldn't tell. Her mind felt like it was wadded with wet facial tissues and she had an annoying itch right in the center of her back.

She longed to reach around and scratch it, but she didn't dare, not while Mr. Morgan was sitting just ten feet away. She tried to look relaxed and comfortable, standing downstage center by the footlights, but it was impossible.

She saw Cody out of the corner of her eye, slumped on a battered sofa that was left over from a production of *Arsenic and Old Lace. He* certainly isn't nervous! she thought irritably. He had been frowning over his script for the past five minutes but lumbered to his feet at Mr. Morgan's command.

"We're ready when you are," Mr. Morgan reminded him. Cody seemed not to notice the sarcasm and stopped to sip a soft drink before taking his place next to Tracy. "You've got the first line, Tracy," Mr. Morgan said, watching her carefully.

Tracy licked her lips. Her mouth felt so dry! She would have loved to have shared Cody's soft drink but didn't have the nerve to ask. She began reading the same lines she had read that first day at tryouts, but somehow the magic wasn't there today. Her voice was flat and colorless, and she winced at the reading. Something was missing, and she knew that Mr. Morgan noticed it, too.

"Stop right there, Tracy," Mr. Morgan said in a surprisingly gentle voice. He eased himself out of the metal folding chair and crossed to her. "Your reading is . . . I don't know, kind of stilted and off-center." He paused and looked at her speculatively. "Are you feeling okay? Maybe you're a little nervous?"

"Yes, a little," Tracy gulped gratefully. As soon as the words were out, she felt like stuffing a sock in her mouth. *That was probably the worst thing I could have said,* she thought miserably. *An actress should never confess to stage fright! How could she have been so stupid?* Her eyes flew to the front row, where Denise was watching her intently.

". . . so I want you to take three deep breaths and try it again." Startled, she realized that Mr. Morgan had been talking to her. She had been so busy concentrating on Denise, she had forgotten that she was in the middle of the most important scene of her whole life.

"I'll try it, Mr. Morgan," she said obediently. She started reading again, but he shook his head and stopped her.

"You're not listening to me, Tracy," he reprimanded her. "I said, three deep breaths."

"Oh, right," she said, flushing. She sucked in three breaths as rapidly as she could and felt a wave of dizziness shoot through her. When she began to read again, she didn't have enough air, and her chest felt so tight she thought it would explode. Her voice was thin and quavery, and Cody looked at her in surprise as she struggled though the lines. Mr. Morgan made a note on his clipboard, and then turned the page, as if he were looking for someone to take her place. She stumbled through the rest of the scene, but it was dry and mechanical, and when she glanced at Mr. Morgan, she thought he looked bored. He looked from the clipboard to the girls in the front row, and Tracy knew that she'd missed her chance. He wanted another Sandy.

"Thanks," he said mildly, when the scene mercifully ended. Cody headed back to the beat-up sofa, and Tracy was left standing alone on the stage. Mr. Morgan adjusted his thick glasses and turned back to his notes, muttering to himself. Tracy felt horribly self-conscious just standing there, but she didn't know what to do next. Should she go, should she stay? she wondered. It was obvious that she wasn't going to give Olivia Newton-John anything to worry about, she thought disgustedly. She'd given the worst performance of her life. The girls in the front row were whispering back and forth, rustling their scripts. They're probably wondering who'll be called next, Tracy thought unhappily.

When Mr. Morgan finally looked up, he looked surprised to see her still standing there. "Oh, Tracy," he said vaguely, fixing her with those piercing dark eyes, "you can take a seat now." He waved to the auditorium. As she moved slowly offstage, she heard him read a name off the clipboard.

Denise Hendrix.

Denise has a lot of style, Jen thought, watching her throw her script carelessly on her chair before heading for the stage. Everyone else clutched the script like a security blanket, but not Denise. She knew the lines cold, and she stood stage center, smiling winningly at Mr. Morgan.

"No script?" he said, peering at her owlishly from behind his enormous glasses.

Denise laughed gaily. "I've got all the lines in here." She tapped her blonde head.

"Are you sure? Because I want to try a scene from the second act. . . ."

"That's fine, Mr. Morgan," she said, her voice clear and confident. "Is it the scene at the Burger Palace?"

"That's right." He looked surprised, and flipped through the pages till he found the scene he wanted. "Page fifty-five," he said brusquely. "I want to see a little toughness here, Denise."

"Okay, Mr. Morgan," she said in her breathless voice.

"Now, Cody," the director began, "you see the new Sandy walk in the Burger Palace, and you nearly keel over, you got that?"

"I nearly keel over," Cody repeated. "I think I can do that." He clutched his heart and staggered backward in surprise, earning a big laugh from the blondes in the front row. Cody grinned impishly. "I think I'm in love."

"Save your jokes for later, Cody," Mr. Morgan said in a tired voice. He looked at his watch and frowned. "At the rate we're going, we'll be here all night." He looked at Denise and motioned her offstage. "Let's see you enter stage right, Denise, and then take a seat right here." He pulled the green metal chair toward the middle of the stage and, with surprising grace, leaped over the footlights. "I want to see how it looks from the audience."

"Should I be sitting or standing?" Cody asked him, edging back toward the sofa.

"How about if you enter from stage left,

Cody? I want both of you to take a few steps and then react when you see each other."

Cody ambled offstage, and Jen's heart thudded with excitement. She grabbed the arms of the plush auditorium seat so hard her knuckles went white, and she held her breath, waiting for Denise's entrance.

When Mr. Morgan snapped his baton a moment later as her cue to enter, Denise had undergone a total transformation. A surprised gasp went up from the hopeful blondes in the front row, and Mr. Morgan turned around furiously to glare at them.

The new Sandy was even more electric than Jen had imagined, and judging from Cody's reaction, he was in a state of shock. Denise strutted across the stage as if she owned the world, and at that moment, no one in his or her right mind would disagree with her. When Cody gasped out her name, she turned those dazzling eyes on him and melted into the folding chair.

Cody was staring at her as if he had seen a vision, and when Mr. Morgan snapped "Line!" he blinked as if he were coming out of a trance. He mumbled through his next speech, never taking his eyes off Denise, and Jen was sure that his reaction was genuine.

Denise looked at him coolly, taking her time before replying. She let a long moment pass before giving him a slow smile of recognition.

When Tracy saw the smile, she knew she was doomed. Either you have it or you don't, Tracy thought mournfully. And Denise, from her perfect legs to her deep blue eyes, definitely had it. Tracy clenched and unclenched her fingers as she watched the stage. She had never felt more helpless in her life. The part she wanted more than anything in the world, the part she was practically *born* to play, was slipping away from her.

Forever.

Chapter 6

A light rain had started to fall when Nora and Tracy pushed open the heavy double doors and emerged on the steps of Cedar Groves High School. Nora peered at the darkening sky, racking her brain for something encouraging to say.

"Want to walk home together?" she said. Not the world's most brilliant remark, but the best she could come up with, under the circumstances.

"Sure." Tracy managed a small, grateful smile.

The school yard was deserted, and the two girls cut across the muddy playing field, trying to avoid the puddles.

Jen and Denise were nowhere in sight. Both girls had vanished the moment the audition was over, arm in arm, all smiles. The two of them are probably out celebrating right this minute, Nora thought glumly. The look of joyful triumph in Denise's eyes had been unmistakable.

"I think it could go either way," Nora began in what she hoped was a positive tone. "You can see how unpredictable Mr. Morgan is," she said seriously. "Anyone who would write in a part for Jason Anthony can't be the most logical person in the world." She tried a light laugh that didn't quite come off, and glanced at Tracy.

"It's okay," Tracy said softly. "You don't have to try to cheer me up." She looked small and fragile in a bright red rain slicker. "I know I blew it. Mr. Morgan would have to be out of his mind to cast me as Sandy. He's found the girl he wants: Denise." She ducked her head against the drizzle, and sidestepped a patch of mud.

Nora was silent for a moment, considering her next move, when someone jabbed her playfully on the arm.

"Hey, you two, want to share my umbrella?" It was Steve Crowley, a dark-haired boy who had been Nora and Jen's friend since kindergarten.

"Just in time," Tracy said, perking up. "I was about to turn into a fuzzball." She patted her blonde hair self-consciously, and Nora had to smile. It's amazing how quickly Tracy's mood can change when a boy is around, she thought wryly.

Tracy and Nora snuggled up close to Steve under the giant black umbrella, and he asked cheerfully, "What are you two doing wandering around in the rain, anyway?"

"Tracy just had call-backs for *Grease*," Nora said, giving her friend a nervous look. Probably the last thing Tracy wants to do is talk about what just happened, Nora decided, but Tracy surprised her.

"Yeah?" Steve looked impressed. "How'd it go?"

"I just can't make up my mind," Tracy said, flashing him a dazzling smile. "Mr. Morgan thinks I'd be just super as Sandy — that's the part Olivia Newton-John played — but I don't know if I really want the part or not." She inched a little closer under the umbrella, her blue eyes wide and serious. "I mean, can you imagine how much rehearsal time would be involved?"

Steve shrugged. "I guess you'd be tied up most nights and weekends," he said vaguely. He was looking at Tracy and didn't seem to realize that Nora was being edged off the sidewalk into the soggy grass.

"That's it exactly," Tracy said. She smiled again, showing her perfect white teeth, and then gave a heavy sigh. "And just think what would happen to my social life! I'd be a real stay-at-home, you know, a . . . stick in the mud." She laughed up-roariously at her own wit, and after a minute, Steve joined in.

Nora felt her foot slide into a giant puddle, and wanted to strangle both of them. *Every time Tracy gets around a guy she acts like an idiot,* she thought angrily. And Tracy had always been attracted to Steve Crowley. She had asked Nora and Jen a dozen times why they didn't want to go out with him, even though both girls tried to explain that you just don't have someone you shared your fingerpaints with for a boyfriend.

"So I think the best thing for me," Tracy was saying in her whispery little-girl voice, "is to take a smaller part. That way, I'll still have the fun of being in a play, but I won't have to give up movies and parties."

Steve nodded sagely, not even noticing that Nora was now trotting clumsily behind them like a dutiful cocker spaniel. Her toes kept banging into Steve's heels, and she had to struggle to keep her head under the umbrella. "That's probably a wise move," he said thoughtfully.

"I'm glad you think so," Tracy said huskily. "I don't need the limelight like some people," she added solemnly. "I don't want to name names, but I think you know who I mean."

Steve digested this information silently.

"You could just give initials," Nora said, but both of them ignored her.

"I'm sure Mr. Morgan will be very disappointed," he said gallantly. "You would have made a wonderful Sandy."

"Why, Steve," Tracy said in surprise, "what a sweet thing for you to say. Yes, I'm sure he will be disappointed," she went on, "but — "

"But I'm sure he'll get over it," Nora said with gritted teeth.

". . . but I'm sure he'll find someone else. Of course, it won't be the same," Tracy said thoughtfully.

"No, of course not," Steve agreed.

Nora seethed silently for a few more minutes, until they reached her house. Steve and Tracy, deep in conversation, started to walk right past it, and Nora jabbed Steve in the back. "Hey, you guys, this is my stop!"

"Oh, sorry," Steve apologized.

"That's all right," Nora said irritably, water dripping down her collar. They walked her to the front steps, and she bolted to the porch.

"I'll try to call you later tonight!" Tracy yelled after her. She threaded her arm through Steve's and winked. "We have tons of stuff to talk about!"

"I can hardly wait," Nora mouthed, the

sound of the rain swallowing up her words.

She hung her dripping coat in the bathroom and wandered into the kitchen, chilled to the bone. "What an unbelievable day," she began, and stopped when she saw Jen sitting at the kitchen table. "Jen!" she said in surprise. "What are you doing here? I thought you'd be —"

"Over at Denise's house?" Jen finished for her. She smiled and dropped a marshmallow into a steaming cup of hot chocolate. "Nope," she said cheerfully. "As you can see, I'm right here, waiting for you." She gestured to the seat across from her. "Grab a cup and pull up a chair. Your mom made about a gallon of hot chocolate before she went upstairs to work on some papers."

"What's up?" Nora said cautiously. She reached for a large brown mug and filled it with hot chocolate before settling down.

"We need to talk," Jen said simply. "I wanted to say something to you today at call-backs, but it wasn't really the right time or place. Not with Tracy and Denise around."

"What did you want to say?" Nora took a tiny sip and stared at her friend.

Jen paused, choosing her words carefully. "Don't you feel like you're in the middle?"

"You mean this whole thing with Tracy

and Denise? I sure do," Nora said feelingly. "Gosh Jen, it's the first time we've ever taken sides against each other, and I don't like it."

"You don't?" Jen looked pleased. "Well, neither do I!" She leaned across the table, her hazel eyes sparkling. "And that's why I think we should form a pact."

"A pact?"

"That's right." Jen nodded her head so vigorously, a lock of black hair escaped from her barrette and tumbled comically over one eye. "I think we should decide right now that our friendship is more important than who gets the part of Sandy."

"Well, of course it is!" Nora said firmly. "We both know that." She looked at her friend and felt a lump rise in her throat. How could Jen ever think that *anything* would come between them? She couldn't imagine not being best friends with Jen.

"I guess I needed to hear you say it," Jen said, her eyes moist. "You know, somebody's bound to be disappointed tomorrow — "

"Probably Tracy," Nora interjected.

"Probably Tracy," Jen repeated, "and I just wanted to make sure you wouldn't hold it against me if Denise got the part."

"Jen, I'd never hold it against you," Nora said slowly. "As far as I'm concerned, the whole thing is over and done with."

They sipped their hot chocolate silently for a moment, and then Jen said shyly, "Friends forever?"

"Friends forever!" Nora smiled and reached across the table to shake hands.

"Now that that's settled," Jen said briskly, "was that Steve Crowley walking home with you and Tracy? I saw you through the front window."

"It sure was," Nora told her smilingly. "And have I got a story for you!"

"Have you seen the new cast list?" Jen said breathlessly to Nora the next day in the cafeteria.

"It's already up?" Nora looked surprised. "I thought Mr. Morgan would take a couple of days to think it over." She paused and glanced nervously at Tracy, who was at the front of the line. "Did, uh . . . ?"

Jen shook her head meaningfully. "Denise got the part of Sandy," she said in a low voice. "But Tracy's not out completely. Mr. Morgan cast her as Marty. That's not a bad part — at least she got some lines."

Nora groaned. "Poor Tracy," she muttered. She pulled a tray from the rack and started to slide it along the rail. "Does she know yet?"

"I don't think so," Jen said seriously. "They just put the list up a couple of minutes ago. But I know one thing. I don't want to be the one to tell her."

"Neither do I," Nora said, her face grim. "But somebody's got to."

"Souvenirs, get your souvenirs!" Jason Anthony's voice boomed through the cafeteria, and both girls jumped. Amy Williams giggled, and Jason darted over to her. "Complete cast lists for *Grease*, for only one dollar!" he yelled, waving a pile of mimeographed sheets.

"How did you get this?" Nora demanded, making a grab for a copy. She looked at Jen. "Omigosh, it's the real list, all right."

"Hey, that's a dollar," Jason said, wounded.

"The cast list was up *last* week," Mia Stevens reminded him. "What's so new about this one?"

Jason grinned. "It's got some important changes on it." He leaned close and snatched the paper away from Nora. "It tells you who got the part of Sandy, and best of all, my name is on it."

"Yeah, I'm really going to pay a dollar to see your name in print," Susan Hillard said sarcastically, pushing her tray past him.

"Wait, there's more!" Jason said. "There's a complete list of the technical crew...."

"I'll give you fifty cents," Mitch Pauley

said, and Jason handed over a paper. He turned to Steve Crowley and Andy Warwick. "Guess what, guys — we're famous!"

Jason started to move down the line, hawking the papers, and Nora lunged at him. "Jason, please don't do this." She grabbed his sleeve and held on tight. "Tracy doesn't even know yet. . . ."

"Doesn't know what?" Tracy said coolly. "Wait, let me guess." She was standing outside the railing, holding her tray in both hands. "I didn't get it, did I?" she said, looking directly at Nora.

Nora gulped. "No, you didn't get the part of Sandy," she said softly. "But there's some good news. You're going to be Marty." When Tracy stared at her blankly, she said quickly, "Don't you remember who she is? That's a really good part, Tracy, and I think you'll be wonderful. . . ."

Tracy stared at Nora for another long minute, her blue eyes welling up with tears. Without a word, she dumped her tray on a nearby table and darted from the cafeteria.

"Honestly, Jason," Nora said angrily. "Now look what you've done!"

"Why do I always get blamed for everything?" Jason complained.

When Nora came home after school that day, her sister Sally greeted her with a hug. "Congratulations!"

"For what?" Nora said wearily. She tossed her books on the kitchen table and collapsed into a chair by the window. She'd been working for hours on an extra-credit biology project, and her back was sore from bending over the lab table.

"For winning a part in the school play, silly!" Sally said happily. "I can't believe it, my kid sister is a . . . performer!" She said the last word in a hushed voice, as if it was a magic password.

"Oh, that," Nora said vaguely. "I knew I was one of the Pink Ladies days ago."

"Well, thanks for letting me be the last one to know," Sally said, putting on a hurt voice. She lowered herself gracefully into a chair, tucking her feet together, yoga-style.

Nora laughed. "It's not like it was a secret, you know. It's just that you've been so busy with dance auditions, we haven't seen each other."

"Not auditions anymore," Sally said gaily. "Rehearsals!" She waited a moment and then added, "I've been cast in the city production of *Swan Lake*."

"Sally! That's great! I'm really proud of you." Nora's enthusiasm was genuine. Even though she didn't share Sally's fascination with ballet, she knew that winning the role meant everything to her sister.

"So we've both got our evenings and week-ends filled up for quite a while," she said slowly.

"Looks that way," Sally said cheerfully. "Oh, by the way, the stage manager called and left a message for you."

"Stage manager?" Nora said blankly.

"From *Grease*," Sally explained, rolling her eyes. "That's how I knew you were in the play," she said. "Anyway," she went on, "they're starting rehearsals a few days early, and they want you at the theater tomorrow."

"Tomorrow!" Nora was so upset, she jumped up, nearly knocking over the fruit bowl. "That's impossible," she said, annoyed. "I've already scheduled some lab time to work on my biology project. I can't back out — I'm right in the middle of growing a culture!" she wailed.

"Well, that's show biz," Sally said, reaching for an apple. "Anyway, they want you there at three tomorrow. Oh, and they said to bring a snack. You'll probably be there till seven or eight."

"Seven or eight!" She thought quickly. Maybe she could get someone to cover for her with the microscope. . . . She was reaching for the phone when Sally interrupted her.

"Oh, and one other thing," Sally said,

"they're working on the first act, and they expect you to have all your lines memorized."

"All my lines memorized," Nora repeated, wishing this was all a bad dream and she could wake up.

"That's right," Sally assured her. She smiled at Nora's stricken expression. "Gee, that sounds familiar. It's not Mr. Morgan, is it?"

"That's him."

"Wow — I worked with him in *The Fantasticks*. Nora, I hate to say it, but you're really in for the experience of your life!"

"It's beginning to look that way," Nora said, returning to the phone. "In fact," she added with gritted teeth, "I may not even live through it."

Chapter 7

When Nora dashed into rehearsal the next day, she found Lucy and Jen giggling together in the front row of the auditorium.

"Hey, where have you been?" Lucy said. "We saved you a seat." She moved her notebook off the chair next to her, and Nora sank into it gratefully.

"I've been trying to do a little work on my biology experiment," Nora explained. She sniffed her hands tentatively and made a face. They definitely smelled like slide fixative.

"And you just couldn't tear yourself away from the microscope," Amy Williams put in from the row behind them.

"That's true," Nora said seriously. "I'm at a really important point in the project. You see, if you don't create the right environment for the culture, with the right lighting, temperature, and — "

"Why did I ask?" Amy groaned. She

leaned over the seat, her brown eyes dancing. "Nora," she said, "you're the only person I know who could worry about a bio project at a time like this." She stared as Nora slid out of her raincoat. "And another thing, you're still wearing your lab apron!"

"Oh, gosh," Nora said, embarrassed. "I wondered why it felt hot in here." She shrugged out of the heavy black apron and folded it carefully on top of her books. "Well," she said brightly, "when do we start?"

A loud crash from a baton against a podium made all three girls jump.

"Looks like right now," Lucy muttered. "His Majesty has arrived."

Mr. Morgan was standing in the center of the stage, surveying the audience with his piercing dark eyes. "Attention, everyone!" he said commandingly. Immediately, the auditorium fell silent. He waited for a long moment before continuing. "Today is an important day for all of us," he began in a deep voice. "For many of you, this will be your first experience with theater, your first time on the stage."

Jen felt a little quiver of excitement go through her at his words. Her first time onstage! This could be a turning point in her life.

Mr. Morgan held the baton behind him

and paced back and forth, his head bowed in thought. "For me it is important, because I will get to know all of you." He looked up and made a sweeping gesture that included the tech crew perched near the footlights and the kids sitting way in the back rows. Then he gave me a little chuckle. "And believe me, when this play is over, none of us will ever be the same."

Yeah, that's exactly what I'm afraid of! Nora thought as she tried to join in the laughter. If Sally was right about Mr. Morgan, the next few weeks were going to be tougher than anyone could imagine.

She listened while Mr. Morgan explained some of the ground rules for rehearsals — no lateness, no chewing gum, no eating or drinking except in certain areas. And of course, everyone had to be letter-perfect in their lines as soon as possible, so Mr. Morgan could start something called "blocking," whatever that was.

The list went on and on, and Nora squirmed uncomfortably in her chair. Her foot had fallen asleep, and she longed to get up to stretch her legs. A couple of times she tried to crane her neck around to see if Tracy had shown up, but the lights in the auditorium were too dim, and the back rows were in shadows. She saw Denise, though. She was sitting off to one side with Cody Miller.

All the while Mr. Morgan was talking, the thin girl who had kept the tryout list at the auditions was watching him intently, making notes on a clipboard. Finally, when he finished his speech, he motioned her to join him at the podium. "This is Sara," he said. "Sara Marshall." He smiled at her and Sara flushed as if she felt more comfortable being in the wings than on the center of the stage.

"Sara keeps track of every aspect of the production," Mr. Morgan went on. "That way, I can concentrate on directing. You'll notice today that I tend to divide people into groups. It saves time, and we accomplish more. For example, I might work with the leads on an important speech" — he gestured to where Denise and Cody were sitting — "while Sara organizes the Pink Ladies for their scene. We also have Ms. Gareth doing the choreography, and Ms. Knight working with the chorus." He paused, letting his dark eyes roam over the audience. "In other words, you should be working every minute you're at rehearsal, either practicing your lines, or learning your song and dance numbers. If you can't find anything to do, you can learn by observing your friends. Now, if no one has any questions, let us begin!"

"I don't think I'm cut out for this," Nora

moaned a couple of hours later. Ms. Gareth, the dance director, had taken the Pink Ladies to a small rehearsal room in the basement, where she was teaching them a jazz combination.

"Now please, girls," Ms. Gareth said appealingly, "don't make this any harder than it has to be." She was a slim redhead in a black and green Spandex exercise outfit. "Three kick-ball-changes, pivot right, pivot left, and a shimmy. This is really a very simple combination." She flipped the music on, and moved effortlessly through a few steps of the opening number.

"Simple if you're a *trained* dancer," Lucy quipped.

"Shall we try it separately?" Ms. Gareth said brightly. "Let's start with you, Ryan." She started to turn the tape deck on, and stopped. "You certainly look familiar. I don't suppose you're any relation to Sally Ryan?"

"She's my sister," Nora muttered.

"Your sister!" Ms. Gareth looked thrilled. "Why, that's wonderful." She smiled warmly at Nora. "You shouldn't have a bit of trouble with this." She flipped a switch and a steady drum beat filled the room. "Take it from the top, Nora. Five ... six ... seven ... eight...."

The next few minutes were the most miserable that Nora had ever spent. She forgot her steps halfway through the routine, and then, in a humiliating finale, tripped over her own foot and landed on the floor. She heard Susan Hillard break up with laughter.

As far as Nora was concerned, "line readings" were the easiest part of the first day's rehearsal. At least we can sit down, she said silently, eyeing the long metal folding table that was set up onstage. She sat between Lucy and Jen, with her script in front of her. There were several girls she didn't recognize, and she assumed that they were high school kids.

"We're just going to run through the opening lines a few times," Mr. Morgan said. "Don't worry about every little word. I really just want you to read for expression, and I want to see how all of you relate to each other." He glanced around the table and scowled. "Okay, we've got Ryan, Armanson, Mann. . . . Where's Marty?"

"That's Tracy's part," Nora said in a low voice.

"That's right," Mr. Morgan answered, as if he'd heard her. "Sara!" he yelled. "Get Douglas. She's in this scene." Mr. Morgan got up to find another folding chair, and Sara scurried off with her clipboard.

"How's Tracy today?" Jen whispered.

"I don't know," Nora said honestly. "She seemed okay when she walked me home yesterday, but I don't know what's going to happen when she runs into Denise."

"It's too bad it had to work out this way," Jen said sympathetically. "I wanted to say something to Tracy at lunchtime, but she never showed up in the cafeteria."

In a moment, Mr. Morgan returned with Tracy in tow. "We'll let it go this time, Tracy, but I don't expect you to keep us waiting again. Got that?"

"Yes, Mr. Morgan," Tracy said meekly, sliding into the chair he offered her.

"Are you okay?" Nora whispered to her.

Tracy nodded, burying her head in her script.

"Now," Mr. Morgan said, adjusting his glasses. "Shall we begin?"

For the next half hour, Mr. Morgan had them say their lines over and over, while he scribbled notes in the margin of his script. Tracy spoke so softly that no one at the table could hear her, and finally the director slapped his hand on the table.

"Tracy," he said, leaning back dangerously on the back legs of his folding chair, "why do I get the feeling you're not really with us today?"

Tracy licked her lips nervously, and

played with her script. "I . . . uh, I don't know, Mr. Morgan."

"Perhaps you're not feeling well," he said in a low voice.

"No, I'm feeling okay." Tracy's voice was thin and hesitant. She looked very fragile in an oversized white sailcloth top, with blonde hair swept back in a ponytail.

"Then perhaps you're already bored with the show?" He smiled like a wolf, showing his teeth.

"No, that's not it at all," Tracy gulped. "I just. . . ."

"You just what, Ms. Douglas?" Mr. Morgan leaned forward and Tracy flinched.

"I just . . . nothing," she said lamely. For a moment there was a pained silence while Mr. Morgan glared at Tracy, and she wound a strand of blonde hair around her finger. Finally she raised her blue eyes to meet his. "I'll do better," she said, her chin thrusting forward. "I'll try to speak up more."

"Bravo," Mr. Morgan said sarcastically. "I thought maybe you were practicing to be a ventriloquist." He looked around the table, but no one laughed.

Later, when the rehearsal was over, Nora caught up with Tracy as she was heading down the center aisle. "Want to stop for a lemon soda? My treat?"

"No, I can't," Tracy shook her head.

"Sure you can," Jen said. "We deserve a break after three solid hours of Mr. Morgan," she added in low voice.

Tracy gave a little smile. "Well, it's awfully late. . . ."

"Fifteen minutes won't make any more difference," Nora said firmly, linking her arm through Tracy's.

"You win," Tracy said with a sigh.

When they were settled at a nearby Cedar Groves hangout Jen decided it was time to set things straight.

"Tracy," she said, pushing the menus to one side, "I never got a chance to explain about Denise. About my helping her with her lines, I mean."

Tracy waved her hand in a tired gesture. "You don't have to explain," she began.

"But I do," Jen insisted. She paused and looked at Nora. "When you and Denise both were up for the same part, it was really tough for us. Nora and I wanted to be loyal to both of you, but somehow, things got all mixed up."

"That's okay," Tracy said. She waited as the waitress took their order. "I admit I wasn't too thrilled at first to hear that you were coaching Denise, but the more I thought about it. . . ." Her voice trailed off and she shrugged. "Well, I figured, she asked you, what else could you do?"

"So you're not mad at me?" Jen asked.

Tracy shook her head. "Nope, not at all."
She clasped her small hands together in
front of her. "If I'm mad at anybody, it's
myself. I wish I had never even gotten involved in this awful play."

"Why?" Jen asked, amazed. "I think the
play's going to be fantastic. I was so excited about the first day of rehearsal I
couldn't even sleep last night!"

Nora smiled. Jen's hazel eyes were sparkling and her cheeks were pink.

"Maybe you're excited," Tracy said de-
spairingly, "but I'm disgusted. Mr. Morgan is a" — she paused while she groped
for the right word — "a monster!" she
said finally. "He's really got it in for me."

"Yeah, I know he was pretty rough on
you at rehearsal today," Jen said sympathetically. She brightened as the waitress
put their drinks in front of them, and took
a giant gulp of her soda. "But you know
something? I think he's just doing that to
scare us. Haven't you ever had a teacher
who yelled on the first day, and then when
you got to know him better, he was really
nice?"

"I guess so." Tracy wasn't convinced. "I
still think he's going to make my life miserable."

"Why don't you tell us what happened
last night with Steve?" Nora said, trying
to change the subject.

"Oh, that!" Tracy looked happier. "I nearly forgot! I was going to call you last night, Nora," she said apologetically, "but it got too late."

"That's okay," Nora said good-naturedly. "I was busy with homework, too. Did anything interesting happen after you and Steve left my house?" Nora shot a secretive smile at Jennifer.

"Anything interesting?" Tracy crowed. "Let me tell you something. I've made up my mind that Steve Crowley is absolutely the cutest boy I've ever seen! I made sure we took the long way home, all the way up Hudson Street, so we'd have more time together."

"Well, don't keep us in suspense," Jen told her. "What happened?"

"Well, we were crossing Vine Street, when the umbrella blew inside out. I nearly panicked, because you know how frizzy my hair gets in the rain, but listen to this: Steve took his jacket off and put it over my head so I wouldn't get wet! Is that fantastic or what? And that's just the beginning," she rushed on.

When Tracy stopped to sip her soda, Nora winked at Jen. What did I tell you? her look seemed to say. Once you get Tracy on the subject of boys, her mood gets a hundred percent better!

Chapter 8

"How'd rehearsal go?" Sally asked brightly the next morning. "Think you'd like to change your plans and become an actress?"

"You've got to be kidding," Nora muttered, sliding into a chair at the breakfast table. "Where's Mom?" she asked. She reached for the orange juice.

"She had an early appointment with a client, so she drove into work with Dad," Sally said. She stood up and began a graceful series of leg bends, holding on to the counter for support with one hand, and a half-eaten piece of toast with the other.

"I don't know how you do that first thing in the morning," Nora said, shaking her head.

Sally smiled, and bent until her forehead almost touched her knees. "It's all what you get used to," she said. "I'd go nuts if I had to spend all those hours in the lab that you do."

"The lab!" Nora exclaimed, glancing at her watch. "I was going to check on my project this morning before class starts. I probably won't have time now."

"How was Mr. Morgan?" Sally asked, her long hair trailing the floor.

"Just like you said he'd be," Nora answered with a laugh. "He really had it in for Tracy. You know how she whispers when she gets upset? He told her he thought she was practicing to be a ventriloquist."

"It sounds like he hasn't changed a bit," Sally said, suddenly popping up. Her face was flushed, and she brushed a stray lock of hair out of her eyes. "Just remember, Nora, if anyone can handle him, you can."

"Hah! I don't think he was very impressed with me."

"You'll be fine," Sally assured her. "Just speak up and don't trip over the furniture. That's the whole key to acting."

"I'll remember that," Nora said seriously. She looked at the clock and scooped up her books. Morning classes, lunch, afternoon classes, and rehearsal . . . with any luck, she'd be back home in a mere twelve hours.

"Hi." The voice was so low that for a moment, Denise almost missed it. When she turned and saw Cody Miller peering down at her, she relaxed and smiled.

"Looks like you're in a hurry," Cody drawled. He seemed to have an endless supply of muscle T-shirts, Denise noticed. The one he was wearing today was navy blue, and he had tucked it into a pair of charcoal denim jeans.

"I'm just going to study hall," Denise said, forcing herself to slow down. Being around Cody made her nervous. He was one of the most attractive boys she had ever seen, and there was that strange resemblance to Jean-Paul. The second period bell had just rung, and they had to push their way down the packed main corridor. "What are you doing here anyway?" she said curiously. "Isn't this a little out of your territory? The high school is next door."

Cody shrugged. "Mr. Morgan asked me to drop off some flyers at the office," he explained. "Anyway, I was hoping I'd run into you."

"You were?" Denise said, pleased. "How did you know where I'd be?"

Cody laughed. "Oh, let's just say I have my sources." When she stared blankly at him, he said, "Okay, I'll confess. My sister, Jane, is in your history class."

"Jane the Brain," Denise said automatically and then flushed. "Gosh, I'm sorry," she said quickly. "I didn't mean that the way it sounded."

"That's okay," Cody told her with a grin. "People never think we're related." He ran his hand through his shiny dark hair. "We don't look anything alike. . . ."

"Noo . . ." Denise agreed, but Cody went on talking.

"And, like I always say, Jane got the brains in the family, but I got the talent." He smiled, to show he wasn't really serious, and Denise's heart went out to him.

"You really are talented," she said softly. "I thought you were terrific at rehearsal yesterday."

"Do you really think so?" he said eagerly. "I don't think I've really found Danny yet, you know? Mr. Morgan thinks I should play him a certain way, but I've got my own ideas."

But Mr. Morgan's the one who's running the show, Denise wanted to say. Instead, she said lightly, "I think there's plenty of time to find the characters. Mr. Morgan said he wouldn't expect too much of us in the beginning."

"He always says that," Cody said grimly. "I've worked in three plays with this guy, and believe me, Denise, he's tough." He paused to let a group of laughing cheerleaders go by. "I was wondering. . . ."

"Yes, Cody?" Denise said encouragingly.

Cody rubbed his chin thoughtfully. "If you're not doing anything right after school, how about grabbing a soda together? There's a lot of things about Danny and Sandy I'd like to ask you."

"Well, I. . . . Sure, that would be fine," Denise stammered. She couldn't believe it — Cody was asking her out! Well, almost. Then her spirits sank. "Wait a minute. What about rehearsal? I'm sure we're both on the list for today." She started to fumble in her notebook for her schedule, but Cody put his hand on top of hers.

"I already checked," he said, "and they don't need us till four. So how about if I pick you up outside as soon as school gets out — say, two forty-five?"

"I — that sounds great," Denise managed to say. She bit her lip, not trusting herself to say anything else. Cody wanted to spend time with her!

"See you then," he said in that low, husky voice. He winked at her and disappeared down the hallway.

Denise stood rooted to the spot, until she heard a burst of giggles behind her.

"Do you know who that is?" she heard a female voice sigh. "That's Cody Miller, the guy who's got the lead in *Grease*. Isn't he just gorgeous!"

"Just gorgeous," Denise said to herself.

* * *

"When I told Andy I was going to be in rehearsal every single night, I thought he'd have a heart attack," Mia Stevens told her friends at lunch that day.

"Well, he knows you have a big part, doesn't he?" Jen said. "After all, Rizzo practically carries the show. She's the one who has all the funny lines."

"I know, but try telling that to Andy," Mia said, rolling her eyes. She had experimented with new green eyeliner, and had woven a few blue strands through her spiky orange hair. She caught Jen staring at her and said proudly, "You like it? I tried for sort of a rainbow effect."

"A rainbow," Jen said weakly. "Yes, I think I can see it."

"A rainbow!" Susan Hillard snorted to Nora. "She looks like a parrot." She paused to butter a roll. "Except, come to think of it," she added, "a parrot would have a better vocabulary." She laughed at her own joke, and then frowned when Nora didn't join in.

"Well, I'm sure Andy will understand," Jen offered helpfully. "After all, he's part of the stage crew, and he'll be working hard after school, too. Did you notice how many guys signed up? It's really nice to see so much school spirit."

"School spirit?" Mia said teasingly. "You've got to be kidding! They just signed up so they could keep an eye on us. Andy admitted it," she said, inspecting a frosted platinum fingernail. "He doesn't trust me around all those cute high school guys."

"He's got nothing to worry about," Susan said. "Most of them wouldn't even talk to us, if it weren't for the play."

"Don't be too sure," Mia said smoothly. "Nick, the guy who plays my boyfriend, has already asked me out."

"Really?" Lucy Armanson asked. "What did you say?"

"I told him my heart belonged to Andy," Mia said dramatically.

"Quick — see if she's got her fingers crossed," Lucy cried.

"I'm not lying," Mia defended herself. "I *had* to say that. Andy was standing right behind the scenery, listening to every word!" Then she giggled. "It's just lucky for me that I noticed his Reeboks sticking out from under a tree."

The lunch period was half over when Denise approached the table hesitantly. "Room for one more?" she asked, balancing her tray.

"Suit yourself." Susan moved her books off an empty chair.

Nora and Jen exchanged a look. This was the first time Denise and Tracy would be around each other since tryouts. What would happen next?

"Well, Denise, how does it feel to be a star?" Susan gave a harsh laugh. "Of course, I guess starring in a high school play is small-town stuff to you, huh? Broadway is more your speed."

"I don't know about that," Denise said smoothly. "I've only seen Broadway plays. I've never been in one." Ignoring Susan, she turned to Nora. "How are the Pink Ladies doing?"

"They'd do better without me," Nora told her. "I think Ms. Gareth is wondering how a dancer with two left feet ever got in the chorus line."

"That's not true," Jen put in. "Nora's doing just fine. And anyway, you'll have the rest of us beat by a mile when it comes to singing, Nora. You've got a really nice alto voice, and you'll be able to belt out those songs."

There was silence for a moment while Denise searched for something to say to Tracy. Tracy seemed to be avoiding looking at her, and her pale blonde hair was falling over one eye as she stared at her plate.

"I hope Mr. Morgan doesn't have any more bright ideas," Denise broke the silence. "He's already asking me to get my hair cut in a bob."

"Never! Don't do it, Denise," Tracy blurted out earnestly. "You've got beautiful hair, and it would be shame to do anything to it." She stopped, suddenly aware that the whole table was listening to her. Susan Hillard had her fork poised in mid-air over her spaghetti, her eyes glittering with interest.

"I think I can talk him out of it," Denise said slowly. She smiled at Tracy. "But thanks for the support."

"Anytime," Tracy said shyly.

Everyone joined in the conversation then, except Susan, who swallowed her meatball in disappointed silence.

"I think it's nice you and Denise have smoothed things over," Jen said to Tracy in the girls' room after lunch.

Tracy was staring at herself in the mirror, carefully applying a fresh layer of peach lipstick. "Well, you know what they say, no one likes a sore loser." She pressed her lips together and added a touch of gloss. "And anyway, we're all friends."

"It's nice that you look at it that way," Jen said seriously. "A lot of people would be disappointed."

"Of course I'm disappointed," Tracy told her. She started brushing her shiny blonde hair. "But I don't think that losing the part of Sandy is so awful, after all."

"No, of course not," Jen said warmly. "Marty is a wonderful part, and —"

"That's not what I meant," Tracy interrupted her. She stood back to study the effect of her new cotton twill jumpsuit. "I don't care about playing Marty."

"Then what in the world are you getting at?" Jen said, puzzled.

Tracy gave her a sly smile. "Well, let's just say I've changed my mind about the boy who plays the lead."

"Cody?"

Tracy nodded. "At first I thought he was the most fantastic guy ever, but now. . . . Well, you saw the way he acted in rehearsal yesterday."

"He seems a little conceited," Jen agreed.

"A little! He acts like he's the only person onstage." She carefully powdered her nose. "Who needs that? As far as I'm concerned, Denise can have him."

"You mean, Cody was the real reason you wanted to play Sandy?" Jen said in amazement.

"Well, he's one of the reasons." Tracy laughed. "I tried out for the play so I could meet a lot of new guys."

"Really?"

"Really. Honestly, Jen, sometimes you are so naive, you amaze me."

Jen's mouth dropped open, but the bell rang before she could reply. She hurriedly scooped her books off the sink and headed for the door. "Coming?"

"In a minute," Tracy said, giving a final tug to her jumpsuit. She smiled at her reflection in the mirror. Losing the part of Sandy might be the best thing that ever happened to her, she thought. This way, she'd have more time to concentrate on the chorus. And there were plenty of cute high school guys in the song and dance numbers. Especially that one with curly blond hair named Joshua Ladd. She was sure that he smiled at her yesterday in rehearsal!

Meanwhile, Denise had become convinced that Cody Miller was the one boy who could make her forget Jean-Paul. By three o'clock that afternoon they were sitting side by side in Cody's beat-up Chevy, sipping chocolate frosteds.

"Some car," Denise murmured, to make conversation.

Cody smiled. "Well, it can't compare with that BMW your brother drives, but it gets me where I'm going." He ran his hand lovingly over the scruffy upholstery. "I hope to trade it in this summer for something newer."

They were silent for a moment, and suddenly they both started talking at once. "About the play," they said in unison. Cody shook his head and Denise started to laugh.

"I guess great minds really do run in the same direction," she kidded him.

"Guess so," he drawled.

"You go first," she offered.

"Well, I was just going to ask you what you thought about Danny," he said, trying to stretch his long legs in the cramped car.

"Hmmm, that depends." Denise paused, sipping thoughtfully.

"C'mon, tell the truth. Do you think I'm playing him the right way? You do like him, don't you?"

"Am I supposed to?" she countered. She looked at Cody's thick dark eyelashes and crooked grin.

"I should hope so!" he said, pretending to be hurt. "Mr. Morgan said that Danny is supposed to be the greatest."

"Wait a minute," Denise said teasingly. "Danny *thinks* he's the greatest. There's a difference."

Cody laughed. "Yeah, I see what you mean." He rested one arm on the open car window. "Well, I was wondering, do you think I come on too strong, too conceited?" He turned to face her, his dark eyes earnest. "After all, I'm kind of rough on you in that scene with the T-Birds. I wonder if I should ease up a little. I don't want the audience to hate Danny in the first act."

"There's not much chance of that," Denise said softly. She found herself edging a little closer on the seat. "You . . . I mean, Danny, is a really exciting guy, and . . . I think he would be a little conceited." She paused. "I think you play him just right."

"You do?" Cody looked pleased.

Denise nodded. "I really do," she said solemnly.

Cody looked at his watch and reluctantly started the motor. "I'm sure glad we're in this together, Denise," he said, backing out of the parking lot. He reached over to playfully squeeze her arm. "You're good for my ego."

Chapter 9

"I need Ryan and Mann onstage," Sara Marshall said, frowning over her clipboard, "and then you, Rizzo, I want you to run lines with Denise. T-birds, get over to dance practice on the double!"

Three weeks had passed, and the rehearsals were starting to follow a pattern. Nora scrambled to her feet. She had been sitting on a battered trunk backstage, her biology book propped on her knees.

Mr. Morgan had been right when he said they'd be busy every minute. There were lines to memorize, songs to sing, and of course, the dance numbers, which Nora still found difficult.

Tracy gave Nora a sympathetic smile as they hurried to take their places. "You look like you didn't get any sleep last night," Tracy said, peering at Nora's pale face.

Nora made a face. "I had to turn in my

biology paper today so I didn't even get to sleep till after midnight — "

"Okay, everybody, listen up!" Sara's voice cut through the babble of voices. Immediately a hush fell over the crowd. "Mr. Morgan wants me to give you a few notes while he works with the lighting crew, so pay attention." She rubbed her eyes and gave a weary smile. "You can make yourselves comfortable, if you want. I'm afraid I've got a lot to go over."

"Great," Susan Hillard said sarcastically. She nudged Nora in the ribs. "Is this fair or what? I'm not even in the play, and I've got to sit and listen to everyone else's mistakes."

Giving Susan a sharp look, Sara said abruptly, "Let's quit wasting time." She adjusted her glasses and turned to Tracy. "Douglas . . ." she began.

"Oh, no," Tracy whispered. "Mr. Morgan has it in for me again. I just know he does."

"I don't quite understand this," Sara said, peering at her notes. "It looks like it says ventriloquist after your name, but it's really hard to read Mr. Morgan's writing."

A sudden bark of laughter from Susan made everyone turn around. "No, that's right, Sara," she said gleefully. "He thinks Tracy is practicing to be a ventriloquist." She laughed and waited for everyone to join in. A few of the high school kids started to smile, and Tracy's cheeks got red.

"I don't think I understand," Sara said, looking bewildered.

"It's simple," Susan explained, delighted at being the center of attention. "Tracy never moves her lips, and she whispers all her lines. Don't you get it? She's just like a ventriloquist."

Sara looked embarrassed. "Oh, well . . . just try to speak up a bit more, Tracy," she said kindly. She ducked her head back to her notes. "Now, let's move along to the Pink Ladies. . . ."

"That's us," Jen muttered.

"Line readings not bad . . . but the chorus numbers are. . . ." She paused and squinted at her notes. "I'm afraid I can't make out the word," she laughed.

"That's probably just as well," Nora said wryly. "I think Ms. Gareth has probably given up on us."

"No, but she's scheduled some extra rehearsal time," Sara told her.

"Extra time?" Nora said weakly. She thought of her lab assignment. At the rate she was going, it would be spring break before she grew the cultures she needed!

"I'm afraid so. She says the dancing is sort of uneven, and you all need more work." Sara shrugged. "Everyone seems to have come from a different dance background. . . ."

"Or no dance background," Nora offered.

"And this is the only way we can bring everybody up to the same level. Now," she said, stopping to take a deep breath, "Rizzo, where are you?"

"Right here," Mia Stevens called. She was wearing a rhinestone-studded jacket over a pair of tight zebra pants.

"Mia, we need you to play Rizzo a little broader."

"Broader?"

"For laughs," Sara explained. "You've got some great lines, and you're supposed to be the craziest person onstage, so . . . act crazy."

Mia hooted. "That should be easy," she said good-naturedly. She turned to smile at Jen. "I'll just be myself. That should do it."

Sara continued with her notes for the next fifteen minutes, until Mr. Morgan appeared onstage. "Well, that wraps up everything I had to say," she told them. "Oh, and one more thing. Jason — please don't bring that skateboard in here anymore!"

"Well, we're getting better," Jen said later at Temptations. She paused to sip her chocolate malt. "I think."

Lucy raised her eyebrows. "What do you mean, you think? Of course we are! My legs will never be the same. I've done so many deep knee bends for Ms. Gareth, I feel like one of those frogs in biology class."

"I do think we're all getting better with the lines," Nora said thoughtfully. "Of course, I'll never get the dance steps right," she added.

"Don't be silly, you're looking better every day. Isn't she, Mia?"

Mia Stevens nodded. "You only stepped on my foot twice today," she said seriously.

Nora groaned, but Jen snapped her fingers and laughed. "What did I tell you — better!"

"Being in the play has certainly changed our lives," Lucy said, looking around the ice-cream shop. It was seven-thirty, and the place was nearly deserted. "Usually I'd be home, and it would be my turn to clean up the kitchen right now."

Nora made a face. "I know what you mean. The only time I eat dinner with the family is on weekends." She stirred her lemon slush and glanced at her watch. "Mom or Dad leaves my dinner in the oven for me."

"You, too?" Lucy started laughing. "Yesterday my little sister pushed the wrong button to warm up my dinner and it cooked on high all over again! It was supposed to be roast chicken."

"Really? What happened?"

Lucy grimaced. "Have you ever seen a chicken that was struck by lightning?"

Mia grinned. "At least you don't have three older brothers who gobble up all the meat and potatoes. Last night, the only thing left was steamed brussels sprouts." She drained the last of her soda. "And you know something? At nine-thirty, they actually tasted good!"

"Well, we all have to make sacrifices," Jen said seriously. "After all, look at Denise and Cody. They spend more hours rehearsing than anyone else."

"Yeah, but it's different for them," Lucy argued. "Cody says he wants to major in drama in college. And I wouldn't be surprised if Denise ends up onstage, too. She's got the looks and the talent."

"Hey, are you saying that we don't?" Mia kidded. "I'm insulted!"

"C'mon, you know what I mean," Lucy said. "The rest of us are just in the play for laughs, and to be honest, I don't think I'll ever do it again."

"How can you say that?" Jen cried. "This has been the most exciting time of my whole life."

"It has?" Lucy finished her soda. "I'll

remind you of that when Ms. Knight has you sing the opening song for the thirty-third time."

"Well, I didn't expect it to be easy," Jen said earnestly. "I knew that being in a play would mean a lot of hard work." She smiled and looked around the table. "But as far as I'm concerned, it's worth every minute!" She stood up and began to gather up her books so she and Nora could walk home together.

"You're really into this," Nora said to Jen as they left Temptations. Jen had turned up the collar of her jacket against the night air and was humming one of the tunes from the show.

"Into *Grease*? I sure am!" She did a little hopscotch step while they were waiting to cross the street, and said, "Isn't it funny how one little thing can change your whole life?"

"What do you mean?" Nora said absently. She glanced down at her bulging notebook and wondered which project to tackle first. History, she decided. Her Napoleon paper was due next week. . . .

"Well, you know, the *Grease* poster!" Jen said. "Just think, if we hadn't seen the poster that day, we wouldn't have auditioned and none of this would have happened."

"You mean I'd be getting better grades and eight hours of sleep?" Nora asked wryly.

"Oh, don't be such a drag," Jen teased her. "You know you're making straight A's. You always make straight A's," she added admiringly. "Even in math — I don't know how you do it."

"Must be through osmosis," Nora said wearily. "Honestly, Jen, it's getting tougher and tougher to get everything done, don't you think? Sometimes I feel that the play is taking up my whole life."

Jen shrugged. "I guess so . . . but when you really love something, you don't mind," she said brightly. "You know what the hard part is going to be?"

"Opening night?"

"No, silly. Closing night." Jen suddenly looked serious. "I can't imagine what I'll do when this is over," she said softly. "Oh well, I'll probably find another play to audition for — some of the high school kids do community theater."

Nora stopped dead in her tracks. "Jen, you can't be serious. Don't tell me you're going to do this again!"

"Well, of course I'm going to do it again. I'm going to be in as many plays as I can." They were in front of Nora's house. Sally, dressed in a pair of red leotards, hurried across the front lawn to her dance rehearsal, giving Nora and Jen a cheery wave.

"I guess I'm just surprised," Nora said slowly. "I don't know what to say." She hugged her books to her chest. "I thought you were in *Grease* . . . just for fun."

"For fun!" Jen looked at her in astonishment. "Nora, I thought you knew how much this meant to me." Her hazel eyes were very bright, and she had a determined look on her face. "In fact, I've decided not to go to college. I'm going to go to acting school!"

"I thought you were wonderful today," Cody said, his dark eyes fixed on Denise. They were parked outside Denise's house in Cody's old Chevy, and a Beatles song was playing on the radio.

"Oh, I don't know about that," Denise said shyly. "I could have done that first scene better, the one where I — "

"No, you were great," Cody interrupted her. A slow smile spread over his face and he ran his hand through his black hair. "So, how about me?" He waited expectantly.

"What do you mean?" Denise was puzzled.

"Well, how did I do onstage?" he said impatiently.

Denise's heart sank. Cody might be the

best-looking boy she had ever seen, but he always turned the attention back to acting. *His* acting.

"I'll tell you what I think," he said, not bothering to wait for her reply. "I'm still not sure about the pacing, you know? Mr. Morgan has me talking so slow, I feel like I'm in slow motion. He says Danny should drag out his lines. He says it's an . . . what's that expression?" He frowned and snapped his fingers.

"An integral part of the character," Denise said wearily. That must be Mr. Morgan's favorite expression, she thought. He'd used it a hundred times already! "If I were you, I wouldn't worry about it, Cody."

"No?" He leaned over and tapped his fingers on the steering wheel in time to the music. "You're not just putting me on?"

Denise shook her head. "You've got to trust Mr. Morgan. He's got tons of experience, and remember, he wants you to look good onstage." Even more that you do, she felt like adding.

"Yeah, I suppose you're right. I hadn't looked at it that way." He reached for his sunglasses, even though it was dark, and Denise giggled. "What's so funny?" he asked, hurt.

"You're really going to wear those? It's almost eight o'clock at night."

Cody chuckled. "Okay, I admit it. I'm a ham." He put on the glasses and peered at himself in the rearview mirror. "If Michael Jackson can get away with it, why can't I?"

Denise started to laugh. There was something so funny and appealing about Cody that she just couldn't resist him. Of course, she knew she wasn't the only one who found him attractive. Some of the high school freshmen were starting to hang around at the rehearsals, just to watch him. . . .

"You're impossible, Cody," she teased him.

"Impossible, huh?" He flashed her a grin. "Then you better watch yourself the day after tomorrow, Denise." He looked amused at her blank expression. "You know what scene we're doing, don't you?"

Denise shook her head. "Something in the second act, I think."

"My favorite scene in the whole play," Cody said dramatically.

"What is it?" Denise was starting to feel a little nervous.

"Check your script," he said mysteriously. "Page forty-nine."

"Page forty-nine," Denise repeated. She had her hand on the door handle, and she felt her stomach rumble. "Not the. . . ."

"The drive-in movie scene!" Cody announced. He leaned forward to switch stations as Denise got out of the car. "It's our big moment, Denise," he kidded her. "You get to kiss me!"

Denise smiled weakly, and started up the walk. The rumble in her stomach had shifted to a full-fledged growl. And it was more than just hunger, she knew. In less than forty-eight hours, she was going to kiss Cody Miller, and she had never been so nervous in her life!

Chapter 10

"Cut!" Mr. Morgan yelled the following afternoon. "Tracy, what in the world is your problem? I've seen better acting from a stick of furniture!" he thundered.

"Uh-oh," Susan whispered smugly to Nora. "Looks like Tracy's in for it."

Nora's eyes remained steadfastly stage center, and her heart went out to Tracy. This was the third time that Mr. Morgan had stopped the rehearsal to yell at her, and Tracy looked like she was about two seconds away from crying.

"What have you got to say for yourself?" Mr. Morgan said, looming over her.

"I . . . I don't know what's wrong," Tracy blurted out. "I knew the lines before I got up onstage — honest."

"Sure. I suppose you could say them in your sleep," he said curtly. He began pacing the stage, his hands thrust in his khaki slacks. "You know, we can't work miracles in rehearsal, Tracy." His voice was harsh. "If you're not going to put in a little practice time at home, you might as well forget it."

"But I *do* practice at home!" Tracy cried. "I rehearse my lines every night in front of the bathroom mirror."

"Good place," Susan snickered. A girl in the chorus giggled, and Mr. Morgan glared at them both.

"I can say them backward and forward at home," Tracy went on, "but something happens when I get in here." Her face was red and flushed and her lower lip was trembling.

"Oh, really?" Mr. Morgan said sarcastically. "And what might that be?"

"I . . . think you make me nervous!" she said defiantly. "I really do. You get me so confused I don't even know what I'm saying — "

"Just a minute," Mr. Morgan said sharply. "This isn't playschool, Tracy." He glanced around at the actors gathered on the stage. "I think everybody else in here knows it. Somehow, you didn't get the message, so I'll spell it out for you. If you can't hack it . . . get out."

For a moment, there was dead silence, and Tracy swayed a little as if she might faint. Then she jutted her chin forward and stared at Mr. Morgan, her eyes blazing. "Good — I'll leave right now!" she cried. "You can keep your stupid play and your stupid part and — " She turned and dashed toward the wings, her shoes making little slapping sounds against the polished stage floor.

For a moment, everyone was too stunned to speak. Jen made a motion to go after Tracy, but Nora shook her head.

"Let her go," she mouthed. "We'll talk to her later."

Mr. Morgan stood staring at the wings, and then snapped his baton against a chair. "Sara!" he bellowed.

"Yes, Mr. Morgan?" Sara Marshall hurried down the center aisle, clipboard in hand.

"You can scratch Tracy Douglas' name from the program," he said loudly. "We're going to recast for Marty."

Sara looked at him in surprise, her pen poised over her notes. "But, Mr. Morgan — "

"No buts," he interrupted. "If anyone has any suggestions, they can talk to me later." He paused and stared at the actors. "Now," he said, letting his breath out slowly, "let's get back to work."

Meanwhile, Tracy was huddled on a battered love seat in the prop room, next to the soda machine. She was dying to go home, but she was trapped for the moment.

Sara had locked the dressing room door, and her purse and books were inside. She rested her head on her hands, wishing that she had never even heard of *Grease*. What a disaster, she thought miserably.

"He was pretty rough on you out there," a husky voice said.

Tracy looked up to see Joshua Ladd, one of the boys in the chorus, looking at her sympathetically. She automatically reached for a tissue, sure that her mascara was smeared all over her face. And her nose! She just knew it was bright red. "Well," she sniffled, "I guess he didn't believe me. But I do practice at home. Really!"

"Hey, you don't have to convince me," Joshua said, sitting down beside her. "I'm on your side."

"You are?"

"Sure I am." He laughed and stretched his long legs out in front of him. "I know what it's like to know something by heart, and then have it fly right out of your head. It makes you feel like a jerk."

Tracy found herself smiling at him, even though she was positive that Joshua Ladd had never felt like a jerk. She had noticed him the first day of rehearsal and had decided he was one of the cutest guys in the play. Next to Cody Miller, of course. But Cody had turned out to be a big disappointment — he might look like Rob Lowe, but he was too conceited. Joshua seemed different somehow. He was good-looking, but he didn't take himself so seriously. . . .

"I can't imagine that ever happening to you," she said. She sat up straighter and pushed her blonde hair behind her ears.

"Believe me, it has. A lot of times." He stood up suddenly and fumbled in his pocket. "Want something to drink?"

"Sure," she said, smoothing her white cotton skirt. "But aren't you supposed to be onstage?" she asked, watching as he fed quarters to the machine.

"Not for a few more minutes," he told her. He handed her a soda and settled back on the couch next to her. "So, what's the next step?"

"What do you mean?" Tracy said, puzzled. She caught herself staring at Joshua's curly blond hair. He's so adorable, and he seems interested in me, she thought happily. Maybe something good had come out of the play after all. . . .

"With you and Mr. Morgan." Joshua stopped to take a giant swallow of his drink. "You'll have to talk to him, you know. If I were you, I'd give him an hour or so to cool off."

"Talk to him!" Tracy was so outraged, she nearly jumped off the sofa. "You've got to be kidding! I never want to see him again."

"Hey, simmer down." Joshua grinned. "I didn't mean to make you mad all over again."

"You're not making me mad," Tracy said, remembering that she probably looked a mess with a beet-red face and a runny nose. "It's just that I'll never get over what happened out there." She paused dramatically. "The man is a monster."

"Sure he is. Everybody at the high school knows that. Even Sara Marshall admits it, and she usually sticks up for him."

"I don't know how she stands him," Tracy said softly. "I think he likes to humiliate people."

"You may be right," Joshua said. He crossed his legs, and Tracy thought that he looked just like an actor she had seen on television the night before. He was wearing a white shirt, open at the neck, with a pair of faded jeans that tapered into a pair of leather cowboy boots.

"Then why put up with him?" Tracy said, irritably. "Why does everyone make excuses for him?"

"Because he's a great teacher and a great director," Joshua said patiently. "Look how much he's done with us. We've been in rehearsal . . . what . . . three weeks, and — "

"Twenty-two days," Tracy corrected him.

"Twenty-two days, then." Joshua continued, "You've got to admire the guy. He took a bunch of kids and he's turning them into actors."

"Not all of them," Tracy reminded him. "He says that I act like a stick, remember?"

"Hey, Tracy," Joshua said, tapping her lightly on the arm. "Don't take it so personally."

"Personally?" She snorted. "That's easy for you to say. He didn't tell you he thought you were a ventriloquist."

"Okay, so he's not subtle," Joshua agreed. "And sometimes he's not even polite. But you've got to admit he's talented." He glanced at his watch. "I'd give him till five-thirty, then I'd go talk to him."

"I told you, I'm quitting the show."

Joshua stood up and drained his soft drink. "A lot of people would be disappointed to hear that, Tracy."

"Hah! I don't think the show will miss me," she said bitterly.

"Don't be too sure of that," he answered softly. "I know I will." He tossed his empty drink can into the wastebasket, and headed for the door. When his hand was on the knob, he stopped and winked at her. "Remember, five-thirty," he said.

For a moment, Tracy was too stunned to answer. He'll miss me! she thought deliriously. He was waiting for her to say something, and she made a gigantic effort to pull herself together. "I'll remember," Tracy answered breathlessly.

By the time Mr. Morgan called for a break a little later, Nora had decided to have it out with Jen. She was still in shock over Jen's decision to skip college and study acting. Who would ever think that her best friend would become stagestruck?

They were sitting side by side in the back row of the auditorium, each cautiously drinking a soda. "You know, Nora, if Sara Marshall sees us with this, we'll be dead on the spot." Jen's hazel eyes were mischievous as she took a tiny sip.

"I know," Nora said tiredly, "but I didn't want to stay in the break room. There's something I want to talk to you about."

"Oh, yeah," Jen said brightly. "Look, I know I stepped on your lines in that second scene today. Gee, I'm sorry. I hate people who do that!"

"It's not about the play, Jen," Nora told her. "Well, actually it is, but. . . ." Her voice trailed off. This was going to be much tougher than she had thought.

"Yes?" Jen said encouragingly.

Nora shrugged. Maybe the best way was just to blurt it out and hope for the best.

"Look, Jen, you really shook me up last night when you said you want to study acting."

"I did?" Jen looked incredulous. "What's wrong with that? Lots of people study acting."

"That's true," Nora agreed. "But I couldn't believe it when you said you're not going to go to college."

"Who needs college?" Jen said lightly. "I'm going to get lots of experience in high school, and then I can head for New York. Or maybe L.A.," she added thoughtfully. "I suppose that would be the best place to do television and movies."

"Television and movies!" Nora looked at Jen's smiling face and felt like shaking her. Instead, she took a deep breath and jumped right in. "Jennifer Mann, that is without a doubt the craziest, most *impractical* thing you've ever said! Do you know how many thousands of people want to do that? Do you know what the odds are?"

"Oh, Nora," Jen snapped, "stop being so practical. You sound like a guidance counselor." She took a furious gulp of her soft drink.

"Well, you need a guidance counselor," Nora retorted. "I can't believe you're making a big decision like this, just because you got a part in a school play."

"It's more than getting a part," Jen

said. "I'm *good* at it." She hiccuped. "Besides, I'm having more fun than I've had in my whole life."

Nora tried to be patient. "Jen," she said slowly. "I'm glad that you're having fun, I really am — "

"Thank you," Jen said wryly.

Nora ignored her and went on. "But you don't look for fun when you're choosing a career!"

"You don't?" Jen said innocently. "Then what do you look for?"

"You look for . . . for a job with responsibility, with a future," Nora said forcefully. "Like medicine," she added proudly. "I know that when I finish medical school I'll be able to work as a doctor for the rest of my life. I'll be able to help people."

"I think that's wonderful," Jen said, her hazel eyes shining. "But medicine isn't for everyone!"

"No, of course not," Nora agreed quickly. "But there are dozens of careers you could go into. You have so many interests." She paused, thinking of all the volunteer work that Jen had done. "I always thought that you'd be a teacher or a social worker."

"When I was little, I wanted to be a zoo keeper." Jen giggled. "Then I thought about being a veterinarian — "

"That's a terrific idea," Nora said approvingly. "You're great with animals."

Jen smiled gently at her. "But now I'm rethinking everything, Nora." She looked around the auditorium. People were moving scenery noisily around the stage, and Sara was huddled over a pile of paper cups with Mr. Morgan. The T-birds were gathered around the battered piano, rehearsing a song, and Denise and Cody were off to one side, working on their lines together. "I guess it's hard for you to understand, Nora." She shrugged. "I never knew the theater was like this. I want to be part of it."

"But Jen," Nora said desperately. "You're letting all this go to your head — don't you see that? You're not spending enough time studying. . . ." A buzzer rang, signaling everyone to be back onstage.

"Oh, Nora," Jen said, standing up. "You may be my best friend. But you know something?" She punched Nora's arm affectionately. "You worry too much!"

Chapter 11

"Now that wasn't so bad, was it?" Tracy Douglas spun around to see Joshua Ladd standing outside the stage door. "I told you he wasn't as much of a monster as you think."

It was six o'clock, and Tracy had just had her talk with Mr. Morgan. It had been brief and to the point. Swallowing her pride, she had assured the director that there would be no more outbursts on her part and that she wanted to be back in the play. Mr. Morgan had stared at her for a moment, and then nodded his head in a kingly fashion. "Fine, fine," he said absently, as if his mind were on more important matters. Surprised, Tracy hastily mumbled good-night, and had just stepped outside the auditorium when she bumped into Joshua.

"It was a snap," she said, still reeling from shock. "I thought he'd give me another lecture, but he just said 'Fine.' It was almost like Mr. Morgan was glad to have me back in the play."

"What did I tell you?" Joshua said happily. His blue eyes crinkled when he smiled, and Tracy's heart melted. She still couldn't believe it: He had been waiting for her!

"You were right," she said, beaming. They started walking down the steps when she had a sudden idea. "Are you finished for the night?"

"Sure am." He jerked his thumb back toward the auditorium. "Everyone's done except the leads. They're working on some big love scene."

"Oh, well, I was wondering. . . ." Tracy felt herself blushing but she forced herself to go on. "Would you like to get a soda or something? I mean, I know you probably have tons of stuff to do — " She felt her heart hammering in her chest. She'd never asked a boy out before, and she didn't know why she was doing it now. It was just that Joshua was so adorable!

"This is kind of a bad night for me," he said apologetically. "My kid brother has a dance recital, and I've got to get him there by seven."

"That's okay, it was a dumb idea," Tracy said, trying to make a joke out of it. So much for taking the initiative!

"No, just bad timing." He grinned at

her. "I'll be glad to give you a ride home, though."

Tracy's heart soared. "That would be ... wonderful," she stammered. Things were working out after all. Joshua Ladd was the most terrific boy she had ever met, and he *liked* her!

Inside, Denise and Cody were still working on the play.

"This is no time to be shy, guys," Mr. Morgan was saying to them. The two leads were sitting side by side on folding chairs, rehearsing the drive-in scene. For opening night, the hulk of a battered Chevy would be dragged onstage, and movie sound effects would blast from the wings.

"I'm not shy," Denise assured him, although nothing could be further from the truth. Her heart was beating so hard, she thought it would rip her chest apart. Why was she making such a big deal out of a simple stage kiss? She glanced at Cody and knew why. She was developing an enormous crush on him!

"Hey, relax," Cody said, pulling her playfully toward him. "You can kiss me on the cheek if you want," he said helpfully. "In rehearsals, I mean."

Denise laughed weakly and bit her lip. "I'll ... I'll do it right this time," she said, earning a laugh from Mr. Morgan and

Sara Marshall. She tried to compose herself, and waited for Mr. Morgan to tap his baton on the floor. The scene called for her to kiss Cody as soon as he put his class ring on her finger. Then Cody would give a line, followed by another kiss. The second kiss was a lot more serious than the first, and Denise found it hard to be cool.

Bang! The baton crashed against the floor and the scene started. Denise took a deep breath and willed herself to be calm. When Cody gave her the ring, she touched her lips lightly to his. So far so good, she thought approvingly. Then it was Cody's turn. He kissed her and her heart did a flip-flop. How could she be cool about a boy like this?

Later, when they pulled up in front of her house, she asked him in. He shook his head regretfully and squeezed her hand. "Sorry. I've got a chem test tomorrow." He tapped his head. "Somehow, the formulas for a dozen amino acids have got to jump from the book to here."

"Well, maybe another time," Denise said, as if she didn't care either way.

"Sure," Cody said agreeably. He glanced at the huge stone house and the carefully manicured lawn. "Another time."

But it was two weeks before she got the chance to spend time with Cody again.

Now she was sitting at the far end of the cafeteria, her eyes glued to the door. It seemed crazy and impossible that Cody Miller would actually appear, but he said he'd meet her there at the one o'clock lunch period. Why he needed to see her was beyond her, but he had seemed so excited on the phone that she was sure it was important. And he had said it was "something that couldn't wait." She had spent half the night trying to figure out what it could be but had finally given up.

She had just about given up when he appeared. "Hi," he said softly, sliding into the seat across from her.

"Hi, yourself," she said in a low voice. She always felt a little shy around Cody. He was so good-looking and so self-assured. It was hard to remember that he was only a couple of years older than she was.

"You're probably wondering what I'm doing here," he began. He put a large manila envelope on the table between them.

"I was a little curious," Denise said lightly. She had dressed carefully that day, in an enormous soft sweater over narrow pleated pants. She had brushed her blonde hair until it fell in soft waves on her shoulders, and she was wearing her new Gucci flats.

Cody barely looked at her, though, and started to rip open the manila envelope. "I need your advice," he said seriously. "I've got to make a big decision today, and you're the one person I can trust."

"Well, I'm flattered." Denise was more puzzled than ever. What kind of advice could she give Cody Miller?

He dumped the contents of the envelope on the table and looked at her expectantly. "Well, what do you think?"

Denise glanced down and found herself looking at dozens of glossy photographs of Cody. They were all head shots, black-and-white close-ups, the size of a piece of notebook paper.

"I had these done by a professional photographer last week," Cody explained, "and I need to decide which one to use for publicity."

"Publicity?" Denise asked. "I thought Sara took care of all that."

Cody shrugged. "Well, she does publicity for the show," he said, "but I like to look out for myself, you know? I don't want to get stuck with a bad photograph. A thing like that can really hurt you, you know?"

"Oh, yes," Denise said, trying to look understanding. "And you want me to help you pick one out?"

"Be my guest," Cody grinned. "Like I said, Denise, you're the one person I can trust."

Denise forced herself to smile, wishing

Cody had at least looked at her. She had gotten up at six-thirty just to iron the pleats in the pants — herself! "Well, let's see," she said, riffling through the photographs. There were smiling shots of Cody, along with dozens of thoughtful shots, laughing shots, and profile shots. "They all look good," she began hesitantly.

"Yeah," he said, pleased. "They sure do, don't they?"

The bell rang then, but Denise made no move to get up. She had a study hall the next period, and it wouldn't matter if she was a few minutes late. After all, Cody Miller had come all the way over to the junior high to see her, and she had no intention of letting him down. She picked up one of the photographs and studied it carefully. "Let's start with this one," she began.

"I tell you I'm in love," Tracy was saying hotly. "And this time, it's mutual."

"Here we go again," Lucy Armanson said, rolling her eyes. "Tracy, remember what you said about Jim Phillips?" Lucy put down her fork and struck a pose. "Let me see if I can remember your exact words. I know 'love of a lifetime' was one of the phrases you used."

" 'The most wonderful boy in the world' was another," Jen said helpfully.

"Nope," Lucy corrected her. "That was

Craig Morrison." She paused. "Or was it Dave Rogers?"

"Okay, you guys," Tracy said, "knock it off." She pushed her diet plate away. "This time is different. Look at me — I'm so much in love I can't eat."

"I'm not sure that proves anything," Nora offered. "You see, Jen got the same thing you did." She pointed to Jen's untouched food. "She's not eating, either, and I know for a fact that she's not in love."

"That's true," Jen said. "It's the soggy cottage cheese. If you took a survey in the lunchroom, you'd find that *nobody's* eating the diet plate today."

"You're impossible," Tracy said disgustedly. "I don't know why you can't understand that this is different. Joshua is . . . special."

"Uh-huh," Lucy murmured. "Are you telling us that you two have gone out?"

"Well, not exactly," Tracy said. "I mean, not yet. You know, with all afternoon spent in rehearsal and everything, who's got time?"

"Hmmm, it doesn't sound like much to go on," Nora told her. "You never see him outside of rehearsal, do you?"

"No, but that doesn't mean anything," Tracy retorted. "We practically *live* in rehearsal. And he did give me a ride home once," she said triumphantly. She didn't dare say that it was the night she had asked him out for a soda.

"Well, I hope it works out for you," Jen said kindly.

"Oh, it will," Tracy said, reaching for an apple. "No doubt about it."

"It's hard to believe," Mr. Morgan said the following day, "but we are just two weeks away from opening night." He stopped pacing the bare wooden stage and pierced the actors with his frightening stare.

"I sure can't believe it," Nora muttered under her breath. If she ever got through the dance numbers, it would be a miracle, she decided. Sally had tried helping her at home, but Nora still had to struggle to keep up with the others.

"Shhh," Jen warned her. She kept her eyes fixed on Mr. Morgan. He was tough, he was impossible, she thought. But he was everything a director should be! He had looked tired the past couple of weeks, and Jen's heart went out to him. It couldn't be easy, trying to whip everything into shape — not just the actors, but the props, the costumes, the publicity. . . . She looked at him fondly. She'd always think of him as the man who had changed her life. The man who had made her realize that she *belonged* on the stage.

Tracy Douglas shifted her weight from one foot to the other, waiting for Mr. Morgan to finish. What a ham! she thought disgustedly. The man is so conceited — he loves the sound of his own voice. Just look at the way he's pacing the stage — pretending to give us a pep talk — when it's just an excuse to hear himself talk. At least there's Joshua, she thought, catching a glimpse of a blond head in the back of the chorus. He made it all worthwhile. . . .

Two weeks, two weeks, Denise said silently. She was perched on an old wooden barrel, next to Cody Miller. They were sitting so close, she could hear him breathing, and unconsciously, she leaned back so that her shoulder was almost touching his arm. Without warning, he leaned forward and his warm arm encircled her. She felt giddy with happiness, and sat perfectly still, afraid to breathe. Cody cared about her! And once this play was over, they'd have time to really get to know each other. Just two more weeks, she promised herself.

Susan Hillard pretended to be listening to Mr. Morgan, but she was actually a million miles away. Her thoughts were churning. She had only two weeks to figure out a way to get Jen out of the play! Then she could step right in! She knew the songs, she knew the dance numbers, and she had the lines down pat. Mr. Morgan was one of those directors who insisted that the understudies be ready to go on at a moment's notice.

The past few weeks had been maddening. She'd had to sit through all these rehearsals as an understudy — a nobody — but now it might all pay off. She stared at Jen, who was watching Mr. Morgan raptly. If only something would happen to her! Susan thought desperately. Something that would force Jen to drop out of the play. The frustrated understudy searched her mind, but came up with a blank. What could it be? She bit her lip in frustration. She had to think of something — and fast.

Chapter 12

"Do you think it still fits?" Tracy asked nervously. She sucked in her breath as Sara Marshall moved a button on her costume. Tracy was standing on a small platform in the dressing room. It was two days before opening night and the air was charged with electricity.

"We can pin it for dress rehearsal," Sara muttered, her mouth full of straight pins. "Let's take a look at the front."

Tracy did a little pirouette in front of the full-length mirror and the red poodle skirt flared against her legs. "Gosh, I can't believe they really wore stuff like this," she said with a giggle. "There's enough material here for two skirts."

"There's enough material there for a tablecloth!" Lucy Armanson hooted.

"You look wonderful," Tracy," Jen said admiringly. Jen was next in line for a fitting and she glanced down at her white cotton blouse and navy skirt. It didn't look very exciting, but Sara had assured her that it was "authentic fifties," right down to the little pearl chain at the neck of her cardigan sweater.

"You really look the part," Nora agreed. Nora had already put on her costume, a green cotton shirtwaist dress with short sleeves. She hated her dress, and was sure that she looked like a dork. She thought of complaining to Sara, but decided not to say anything. After all, Nora thought happily, by next week, the whole thing will be over. She thought fleetingly of her biology project, neglected slides filed away in the lab. I'll probably have to throw out my results and start all over, she mourned silently.

Sara rushed through the next fittings and, after consulting her clipboard, said wearily, "Susan Hillard. We'll need to make sure you can wear Jen's outfit, as understudy. And has anyone seen Denise? I need to work on her second act costume."

"I'm here, Sara," a calm voice announced, and all heads swung to the doorway. "I put something together myself, and I want you to see if it's okay."

Denise was wearing a long khaki trench coat and Sara looked at her dubiously. "Well, it better be sensational," she warned, "or we'll have to go with the stirrup pants outfit." She motioned to a pair of red stirrup pants and a tube top that were hanging on a garment rack, left over from last year's production of *Li'l Abner*.

"I think this looks better than what we had," Denise insisted, making her way to the platform.

"Well, get up here and let's take a look," Sara said. "But I'm not making any promises. Mr. Morgan has already approved the stirrup pants, you know, and —" She broke off as Denise dropped the trench coat to the floor and a gasp went up in the room.

"Denise!" Jen said softly. "You look terrific! Doesn't she look wonderful, Nora?"

Nora nodded. Even her worst enemy would have to admit that Denise was a knockout. She was wearing a skintight unitard of black Spandex, topped by a white off-the-shoulder sweater. The combination of black and white accented her honey-blonde hair and made her skin glow. She'd completed her outfit with little slingback high heels.

Sara clapped her hands together delightedly. "I love it!" she cried. "How did you do it, Denise?" She slowly circled Denise, checking every detail, "It's absolutely perfect. Mr. Morgan will adore it."

"I just wasn't happy with the red stirrup pants," Denise explained. "I know you did the best you could, with no budget," she explained. "So, it's going to be okay?" Denise concluded shyly.

"It's more than okay, it's sensational," Sara told her. "Now get off that platform so I can get back to work," she ordered with a smile. "I've got to figure out a way to make all the other costumes look as good as yours," She pushed her horn-rimmed glasses on her nose and checked her book. "Hillard, are you here? Let's see how you look in Mann's costume."

"I'm a nervous wreck," Nora muttered the following night. They had just finished dress rehearsal, and were sitting onstage, waiting for Mr. Morgan to give them their "notes." He was sitting in the first row, huddled over a clipboard with Sara Marshall, and from the look on his face, things weren't going too well. Sara was talking earnestly to him, making little fluttery gestures with her hands.

"Look at Sara," Mia Stevens murmured. "She's probably making excuses for us."

Lucy giggled. "She's got her work cut out for her then, because we were *hor-ri-ble* tonight." She drew out the word to three syllables, and Jen laughed.

"Well, you know what they say," Nora offered. "Bad dress rehearsal, great performance."

"You're just making that up," Mia countered.

"No, I'm not," Nora insisted. "My sister

Sally's a dancer, and she says it's true."

"Well, I hope she's right," Lucy said, instinctively drawing closer to her friends. "Because Mr. Morgan's getting up, and I think we're *in* for it!"

"Okay, boys and girls," Mr. Morgan said, bobbing up from the orchestra pit. "You might as well get comfortable because we're going to be here for a while." He paused and studied the group, his expression cold. "A *long* while. . . ."

Much later, Denise and Cody were driving to Luigi's to get pizza for the group. "I can't believe it's nine-thirty," Denise said. "It seems like the rehearsal is going to last forever."

"It's the last night before the play," Cody said lightly. "I figured it might be an all-nighter."

"Really?" Denise said incredulously "But we've got school tomorrow."

Cody laughed. "Hah! Tell that to Mr. Morgan. Remember that line from Shakespeare he's always quoting? 'The play's the thing'? Well, he really believes it. To him, the play *is* the thing." He shrugged. "I guess it's what makes him a great director."

"I guess so," Denise said dubiously. They had never taken plays this seriously at her school in Switzerland, and she couldn't get used to it. She tried to cover a yawn and said, "Well, it's been an experience, hasn't it?"

"It's been a *terrific* experience," Cody said in his deep voice. They stopped at a traffic light, and he surprised her by reaching for her hand. "I never thought I'd find such a dynamite leading lady."

"Why, Danny," Denise said, lapsing into her Sandy character. "You're going to make me blush." He smiled at her, and her heart did a flip-flop. Not only was he the most fantastic-looking boy she had ever met, she thought happily, but they had so much in common. And it was all because of *Grease* that they were together. . . .

"Hey, don't blush yet," Cody said in Danny's macho style. "This is just the beginning."

Just the beginning! Denise was glad that the car was dark. She was positive that her face really was bright red, and her hand trembled a little in Cody's. "Whatever you say, Cody," she said softly.

Meanwhile Tracy was wandering around the auditorium, looking for Joshua. He had disappeared right after Mr. Morgan announced the break, heading toward the dressing room. Tracy was making her third trip to the basement when he bumped into her.

"Hey," he said cheerfully, "just the person I want to see."

"And why would that be?" Tracy said, flirting happily.

"Well, who else would I split a chocolate soda with?" he said innocently. "What do you say we head for the break room and relax?"

"Sounds great," Tracy said eagerly. She had been dying to see Joshua for days, but their rehearsal schedules had kept them apart. If only this stupid play were over! Then they would have all the time in the world to be together. . . .

Joshua must have been thinking the same thing, she decided, because as soon as they settled themselves on the battered sofa, he grinned at her. "So," he said, "one more night to go."

"I can hardly believe it," Tracy said breathlessly. "Everything will change once the play is over," she said, giving him a hint.

"Oh, not as much as you think," he told her. "Some things never change."

They were interrupted then, when some of the cast came crashing into the break room, full of noisy laughter. Tracy could have cheerfully killed all of them.

"Are you sure about that?" she asked softly.

Joshua looked puzzled. "Of course I am.

As soon as this play is over, there'll be try-outs for the next one."

"Oh," Tracy said, disappointed. She was sure that Joshua had been talking about *them*! Someone asked Joshua for a quarter then, and she tucked her legs under her and watched him while he chatted with his friends. A few minutes later, he winked at her, and she felt her spirits soar.

It was obvious that Joshua felt very strongly about her. She could hardly wait to have real dates with him, instead of these hurried meetings in the break room. Maybe they'd even go steady!

"What do you think? Will we make it?" Nora asked Jen at eleven-thirty that night. She was curled up in bed, her princess phone tucked under her ear.

"If I can hit that high C in the first song, we'll make it," Jen teased her.

"And if I can get that three-step turn right," Nora moaned. "Did you see what I did tonight? I still turned to the left instead of the right. I felt like such an idiot!" She clutched the covers under her chin, embarrassed at the memory.

"Oh, Nora," Jen consoled her. "You worry too much. I don't think anyone even noticed."

"The girls in the dance number noticed,"

Nora said darkly. "And what about Ms. Gareth? If looks could kill, I'd be in my coffin."

Jen giggled. This was the best part of the day, she thought sleepily. Comfy and warm in her new Garfield pajamas, talking to her best friend. "Well, I'm sure you won't make the same mistake on opening night," she said encouragingly. "Just think *right*."

"I wish I could program myself like a computer," Nora said with a sigh. "Or better yet, get a robot to stand in for me in the dance numbers."

"Isn't it nice the way everything worked out?" Jen said dreamily, twisting the phone cord around her fingers. "Denise and Tracy aren't mad at each other. . . ."

"And they each got a part in the play," Nora pointed out.

"And they both found cute boys," Jen said with a giggle.

"You mean it's true?" Nora said, surprised. "I thought Denise was spending a lot of time with Cody. . . ."

"They spend every minute together at rehearsals," Jen said solemnly. "And I saw Tracy and Joshua together today. They're such a cute couple."

"Looks like we're the only ones who didn't end up with boyfriends," Nora said with a laugh. Actually, that was fine with her, she thought feelingly. She'd never be able to juggle school work *and* the play *and* a boyfriend!

"I ended up with something more important," Jen said mysteriously.

"You did?"

"Sure I did." She paused. "I found out what I want to do with my whole life!"

They talked for a few more minutes until Nora felt the phone slipping from her fingers. "Uh, Jen," she muttered. "Do you think we could continue this conversation tomorrow?" She gave an enormous yawn and slipped down under the covers.

"Whatever you say, Nora," Jen said. "Except I hate to tell you — it's after midnight. Tomorrow's already here!"

"Break a leg!" Jason Anthony shouted to anyone who would listen. It was six-thirty on opening night, and the backstage area of the Cedar Groves High School auditorium was a madhouse. Jason was whizzing past the dressing rooms on his skateboard, sure that Sara Marshall would have too much on her mind to bother with him.

"I can't believe you brought that in here," Jen said. She flattened herself against the wall as Jason skidded by.

"Hey," he called cheerily over his shoulder. "It's my good-luck charm."

140

"With a face like that, he'll need it," Susan Hillard remarked. She smiled at Jen, who was standing alone in front of the makeup mirror. "How are you doing?" she said in a friendly voice.

"Why, I'm just fine," Jen said, surprised. This was the first time in weeks that Susan had bothered to talk to her.

"You mean you're not nervous?" Susan smiled. "Not even a little tiny bit?"

"No, I don't think so," Jen said, brushing her hair. She stared at Susan in the mirror. "Of course, I've got a few butterflies. . . ."

"I thought so." Susan nodded knowingly. "First night jitters. It happens every time."

Jen's mouth suddenly felt dry and she licked her lips. "Well, it's not jitters exactly. It's more like excitement," she said carefully.

"Your voice is a little shaky," Susan said kindly. "I hope you'll remember to speak up. You know how Mr. Morgan always says to play to the back of the house."

"Oh, I'm sure — I'm sure I'll be fine," Jen said bravely. The funny thing was, her voice *was* starting to sound a little quavery. She rubbed her hands together and was surprised to find that they were damp.

"Sweaty palms," Susan said crisply, looking over her shoulder.

Jen quickly rubbed her hands on her dress and turned her attention back to the mirror. Her heart was starting to beat a staccato rhythm in her chest, and she forced herself to take several deep breaths.

"I remember when my cousin Charlotte was onstage in her first play," Susan said, sitting on the counter. "Gosh, everyone was so excited for her. The whole family came to opening night." She paused. "All her friends, too. People she hadn't seen in years."

"My family's here tonight," Jen said proudly.

"That's nice," Susan said, her voice soft and wheedling. "Of course, it wasn't so nice for Charlotte."

"No?" Jen was starting to get worried.

"No, I'm afraid not." Susan gave a sad little chuckle. "She had one of the worst attacks of stage fright I've ever seen."

"Stage fright?" Now Jen was really alarmed.

Susan nodded sympathetically. "She was in absolute terror. Yes, *terror*," she repeated and waited for the word to sink in. "All the lines she had memorized flew out of her head, and she just stood there, staring at the audience."

"How awful!" Jen cried. "What did she do?"

"What could she do?" Susan said softly.

"She was rooted to the spot, just like a tree. There was dead silence, and then...." She paused dramatically.

"Then what?" Jen said desperately.

Susan looked at her for a long moment. "People in the audience started laughing," she said slowly. "First the people in the front row, and then the middle rows, and the back rows. All her friends and relatives ... the whole auditorium just cracked up."

Jen's face was a mask of horror. "How ... how awful," she said in a strangled voice.

"Yes, it was." Susan slid off the counter, a sly smile on her face. "The director had to walk out and lead her off the stage. Of course, that would never happen tonight," she added cunningly. "Not here. Not with you."

Jen opened her mouth to say something and then closed it abruptly. Her chest felt tight, and her heart had increased its crazy thumping. Stage fright? It couldn't be happening to her!

"Well, I better be going," Susan said, heading for the door. "Like they say, break a leg!" She paused and looked at Jen's reflection in the mirror. A pale, frightened face gazed back at her. She smiled sweetly and stepped out into the hall.

Chapter 13

"I thought I'd never get here," Nora said breathlessly. She threw her tote bag down on the counter in the girls' dressing room and turned to Lucy Armanson. "First Sally was going to give me a ride, and then she got a last minute call from a choreographer . . . so Mom decided to drive me, but she had to stop and get gas . . . and then we stalled at a red light!"

"Hey, slow down," Lucy said, chuckling. "Look at you. Your face is bright red." She dragged a wooden stool over to the mirror. "Why don't you have a seat and relax until it's time for makeup."

"Good idea," Nora said, collapsing into a chair. "So, what's the plan?" she said, glancing around the crowded room. Several girls were wriggling into their costumes while others were rehearsing their lines.

Lucy consulted a typewritten sheet posted on the mirror. "Let's see, everyone should be in costume by seven . . . and Sara Marshall and her crew will do the makeup when she gets here. I suppose she'll do the main characters first," she said thoughtfully. She grinned. "After all, we're only minor characters. The people in the back row will have to squint to see us!"

Nora laughed, some of the tension easing out of her. "Where's Jen? I thought she was going to get here early."

"I don't know," Lucy asked, frowning a little. "It's funny but I haven't seen her tonight."

"I did," Tracy offered. "Sara must have sent her on an errand. I saw her down in the prop room . . . but that was ages ago."

"But all the props are already onstage," Nora pointed out.

"Don't ask me," Tracy said with a shrug. "I'm sure she'll turn up soon." She whirled around, admiring herself in the full-length mirror.

Nora hesitated. She felt a little tingly feeling at the base of her spine. Something was wrong . . . but what?

A few minutes later, she had her answer when she raced downstairs to the prop room and found the door ajar. "Jen," she called softly. "Are you in here?" She groped along the wall, looking for the light switch. When she found it, she gasped aloud. "Jen!" she cried.

"Just go away," Jen said dully. She was sitting on a steamer trunk used in *Arsenic and Old Lace*, and her face was tearstained. "And shut the door after you." She wiped her eyes with the sleeve of her sweater. "I'm staying here till after the play is over."

"Jen, what in the world are you talking about? What's wrong?" Nora rushed to her friend's side and took both of her hands in hers. Jen's hands were like ice.

"I can't . . ." Jen mumbled.

"You can't what?" Nora sat down, perplexed.

"I can't go out there!" Jen blurted out. "I can't go on that stage."

"But Jen. . . ." Nora didn't know what to say.

"And you can't make me," Jen said defiantly. "Anyway," she said, sniffling a little, "what would be the point? Mr. Morgan would just have to come and lead me off."

Now Nora was more puzzled than ever. "Lead you off? Why would he do a thing like that?"

"Because I'm going to forget my lines," Jen said promptly. "All of them."

Nora laughed. "Are you kidding me? Of course you're not going to forget your lines." She tried a joke. "Just think what

146

a disaster that would be — Susan Hillard would have to take your place." As soon as the words were out, a thought struck her. "Did Susan say something to you?" Nora asked sharply. "Have you seen her tonight?"

Jen nodded. "She told me about her cousin, the one with stage fright." She looked at Nora, her eyes wide and frightened. "Nora, it was awful. You can't imagine what happened to her. The audience was laughing, and she was frozen to the spot. . . ."

"I knew something like this would happen," Nora muttered. "Get up, Jen," she said firmly. "This has all been a trick."

"It has?"

"That's right. A nasty trick." She pulled Jen to a standing position. "I'm going to prove something to you." She took a few paces back and struck a pose.

"What are you doing?"

"Act one, scene two," Nora said promptly. "I want to hear your lines."

"I can't!" Jen said wildly.

"Yes, you can," Nora promised. "Because I'm going to stand right here until you say them. C'mon, I'll give you the first cue. . . ."

"Nora," Jen said pleadingly.

"No excuses!" Nora snapped. "I'm going

to prove to you that you know those lines, and this is the only way I can think of to do it!"

"Wish me luck," Tracy said gaily a half hour later. It was just fifteen minutes to curtain time, and she spotted Joshua standing alone in the wings.

"You're supposed to say break a leg," he reminded her gently.

"Oh, that's silly," Tracy retorted, spinning so he could get the stunning effect of her full skirt. "What do you think — do you like my costume?"

"Sure," Joshua said politely. He turned his attention back to the technical crew, who were rehearsing some lighting cues behind the closed curtain.

"Boys," Tracy muttered under her breath. As far as Tracy was concerned, she wouldn't care if the entire lighting crew dropped through the stage floor. But she reminded herself that there would be dozens of cute boys in the audience, not that she was looking for anyone else, but it never hurt to keep your optinos open. . . .

Meanwhile, Denise was watching the darting spotlight, wondering if anyone else could hear her heart pounding. She was leaning against a wardrobe chest backstage, and she jumped when Cody's arm encircled her.

"Take three deep breaths," he ordered her.

"Three deep breaths?" She turned around so she could face him.

"That's the standard cure for stage fright."

"Who says I have stage fright?" she asked, locking her fingers through his.

Cody smiled. "I could hear your heart beating all the way across the room.

"You could not!"

"Okay, I couldn't," Cody confessed. "It was just a lucky guess."

Denise laughed then, and relaxed a little. She knew everything would be okay. She was going to be onstage with the most terrific boy in the world — he was smart and funny and a wonderful actor. What could go wrong? Cody must have read her thoughts because he planted a little kiss on the top of her head.

"I'll be right there with you, Denise," he said softly.

Denise looked at him, her blue eyes sparkling with happiness. "Oh, I know, Cody. I know!"

Sara Marshall was frantic. She ran breathlessly down the hall, and tagged Jason Anthony, who was inspecting the wheels on his skateboard.

"Is there a problem with Jennifer

Mann?" she gasped. "I just heard that she can't go onstage."

"Hey, I'll take her place," Jason kidded. "Just give me a minute to change my costume."

Sara pushed him aside and threw open the door to the dressing room. Jen was holding a cold cloth to her eyes, and Nora was sitting by her side. "Jen," Sara said, her voice tight with concern. "Susan Hillard told me you can't go on. She wants your costume for the opening number."

Nora gave Jen a what-did-I-tell-you look and slowly got up. "Well, I don't know why," Nora said quietly, "because Jen's going on tonight."

Sara looked from Nora to Jen, taking in Jen's red eyes and pale skin. "You're sure you're okay?" she said worriedly.

Jen reached over and squeezed Nora's hand. "I'm more than okay," she said firmly. "I'm going to be terrific!"

"Fifteen seconds," Sara Marshall hissed. The actors were standing backstage in complete darkness, listening to the band belt out the opening number. They were motionless, frozen like a tableau. "Ten . . . five . . ." Sara turned and flashed a big grin. "You're on, gang!"

Suddenly the heavy curtain started to go up. It moved with agonizing slowness, while the cast waited with smiles plastered on their faces. Jen felt a moment of blind panic. What if Susan was right — what if I forget my lines?

She clutched Nora's arm, terrified. Nora looked at her, and knew immediately what was wrong. She leaned over and whispered a few words in Jen's ear. It was her cue for her first speech. Jen stared at her for a moment, her eyes wide with fright. Then she slowly relaxed and silently mouthed her reply. It was going to be okay. She knew her lines!

The first two scenes went by in a blur, and suddenly it was time for the "Summer Nights" song. Nora, Jen, and the other Pink Ladies stayed at the far end of the stage while a spotlight came up on Cody.

He looked terrific. Denise watched him out of the corner of her eye. He was surrounded by his friends, the T-birds, as he sang and danced, telling the guys how he first met Sandy.

Then it was Denise's turn to step into her own spotlight. With the Pink Ladies gathered around her, she gave her own version of their meeting. Naturally, it was very different from Cody's, and the audience laughed through her lines.

Finally the scene ended, and Nora, Jen, and Mia darted offstage for a quick costume change. Sara had created a makeshift dressing room for them backstage, by hanging a sheet over a curtain rod, and all the Pink Ladies ducked under it.

"How much time do we have?" Lucy whispered, wriggling out of her cotton dress. She reached for her next costume, a pink flannel nightgown and large fuzzy slippers.

"Not much," Nora hissed back. "They're already doing the next song." This was one of the tightest costume changes in the show, and the girls had just minutes to dress for their "pajama party" in the next scene.

"How do you think it's going?" Mia Stevens asked. As Rizzo, she had the wildest outfit, a pair of bright red pajamas with "Atlantic City" plastered on the front.

"You were great," Jen said. "Everybody loved that scene in the cafeteria."

"Hey, speed it up, you guys," Sara said, sticking her head under the sheet. She looked at the stopwatch she wore on a chain around her neck. "You've got a minute and a half." She paused, sitting on her haunches. "How's it going out there?"

"It's terrific," Nora told her. "Aren't you watching us?"

Sara made a face. "I've got to stay backstage tonight and keep an eye on the technical crews. Some of those lighting changes are pretty tricky." She sighed and tucked a strand of brown hair behind her ear. "Maybe someday I can sit out front." She started to duck back under the curtain and stopped. "But hey, you're not alone out there. Mr. Morgan's sitting front row center. He won't miss a thing!"

"We know," Jen said to a chorus of chuckles.

The rest of the scenes passed quickly, and at the end of the first act, the curtain came down to thunderous applause. The moment the curtain touched the dusty stage floor, Cody enveloped Denise in a bear hug.

"Do you hear that!" His voice was triumphant. "They loved us!" He grabbed her elbow and steered her over to the wings. "Let's get out of here for a few minutes. I've got to get a breath of air."

"But we're not supposed to leave the building," Denise protested.

"Who says we're leaving the building?" he said, flashing his dazzling smile. "C'mon!" He pulled her into a workroom on the second floor and cranked open a full-length window. "There's a balcony out here," he explained.

Denise stepped out into the balmy night air. It was a starry night, and she had never felt more happy in her life. She looked at Cody, who was leaning against a wrought-iron railing, the breeze ruffling his dark hair. "Just like *Romeo and Juliet*," she said softly.

"What?" He looked preoccupied.

"*Romeo and Juliet*," she repeated. "You know, the love scenes."

"Oh, yeah," he said abruptly. "Denise, I've been thinking about something," he said, his voice serious.

"You have?" She took a step closer to him. Maybe this *would* be like *Romeo and Juliet*. . . .

He nodded. "I was thinking of making a change in my speech in the second act."

"Your *speech*?" She couldn't believe it!

"The one in the drive-in movie. I think some of those lines would be funnier if I face the audience, you know? I know Mr. Morgan didn't block it that way, but I think it would get more laughs if we did it like this. . . ."

For the next few minutes, Denise listened politely as Cody went over his ideas. She found that Cody didn't need much encouragement. As long as she nodded or murmured from time to time, he was happy to do all the talking. The trouble is, she thought disgustedly, he wants to talk about the play, and I want to talk about something more important. Us!

An hour later, the curtain came down after the finale, and the whole cast gathered onstage to take their bows. Hands linked together, Jen and Nora danced out with the Pink Ladies. They waved to the audience amid wild clapping, just as the T-birds strutted out to take a bow.

"We did it, we did it!" Nora whispered to Jen. She couldn't believe she had actually gotten through the dance steps. Well, almost. She had made one tiny mistake in the first number, but she was sure no one had noticed.

Jen smiled back at her and then they hurried offstage as Denise and Cody swept out, arm in arm. They look great together, Jen thought. I'm so glad that Denise has found someone. . . .

Meanwhile, Tracy was standing in the back row with the other chorus members. They had taken their bows first, all together. Unfortunately, she and Joshua were at opposite ends of the stage, but she was determined to catch him afterward and give him a big hug. She'd have the perfect excuse — not that she needed one! She smiled prettily at the audience and hoped there wouldn't be any more curtain calls to keep her from Joshua.

Chapter 14

For a long moment, Nora and Jen just stared at each other. The curtain had come down for the last time, and the cast members were ecstatically hugging each other backstage. Giggles and shouts rang out as Sara Marshall darted out from the wings, warning everyone to keep it down.

"Well, you made it," Nora said softly, and then Jen grabbed her in a huge bear hug.

"I sure did!" she cried. "And it was all thanks to you." Her hazel eyes were moist, and she clasped Nora's hand very tightly.

"Hey, you would have been fine without me," Nora said lightly.

"No way," Jen answered feelingly. "Susan Hillard really got to me. If it hadn't been for you, I'd still be hiding back in that storeroom. You pulled me through."

"Anytime," Nora said with a shrug. Then she giggled. "Tell me something.

Could you really picture yourself being led offstage by Mr. Morgan?"

"That's what made it so awful!" Jen said, nodding vigorously. "It would be bad enough to forget my lines, but to think of Mr. Morgan coming to get me. . . ."

"What do you think, guys?" Mia Stevens said suddenly, throwing an arm around their shoulders. "Were we cool, or what?"

"Want my autograph now?" Jason jumped up behind them. His face was streaked with orange makeup, and he scrubbed it with a paper towel. "What a mess!" he muttered. "I hope this stuff comes off. I don't want to go to the cast party looking like a carrot."

"You already look like a carrot," Lucy Armanson said, reaching over to mess up his red hair. "And what's this about a cast party?"

"Don't you people know *anything*?" Jason said, drawing himself up to his full height. "Mr. Morgan's throwing a cast party for us downstairs in the makeup room. He's got food and everything down there."

"He does?" Nora said in surprise. "I thought we'd all get together and go to Temptations."

"Don't be silly," Lucy told her. "We can always do that." She grinned. "How often

157

do we get a chance to go to a high school cast party?"

"Listen," Jason said, holding up a hand for silence. In the distance, they could hear the steady thump of a rock song. "We better get moving. The party's already started!"

Tracy smiled at her reflection in the dressing room mirror and reached for a tube of peach lipstick. She looked pale under the harsh makeup lights, with her face scrubbed clean of greasepaint.

"Hey, Tracy," Mia Stevens said, "aren't you ready yet? All the food will be gone."

"That's okay," Tracy told her. "You guys go on without me. I just need a couple more minutes."

"What for?" Lucy Armanson said curiously. "The play's over. We can relax." She pulled a bright red T-shirt over her faded jeans and fluffed out her black curls. "It feels good to get back in our own clothes. I couldn't have lasted another minute in that poodle skirt and crinolines."

Tracy smiled vaguely, her mind on the party. She looked at the pale yellow angora sweaterdress hanging on the garment rack. It had looked perfect at home, but now she was having second thoughts. Maybe she should have gone for a more casual look — a jumpsuit or her best jeans? She wanted everything to be perfect tonight. Joshua is out there waiting for me, she thought happily.

"Honestly, Tracy," Nora said impatiently. "You'd think you were going back onstage."

"I told you to go ahead," Tracy answered in her whispery voice. She brushed her long blonde hair back and fastened it with white barrettes. She turned to smile at her friends. "I'll be out there in a minute, okay?"

"Whatever you say," Lucy said, heading for the door. "This is my first high school party, and I don't want to miss a minute."

As soon as everyone filed out, Tracy reached for her dress and pulled it over her head. She stared at herself and breathed a sigh of relief. The dress was perfect. Thank goodness she had made the right choice. She and Joshua would probably only spend a few minutes at the cast party. They might go somewhere for a quiet dinner, or maybe even try that new disco down on Front Street.

The cast party was crowded when Tracy finally made her entrance. She reached for a soft drink and started to make a slow circle of the room. She was glad she had worn the yellow dress, she decided. Most of the girls were wearing jeans or pants, and Tracy always liked to be different.

Anyway, most boys preferred girls to wear skirts. She had just read that in a teen magazine. . . .

"Going to the prom?" Jason Anthony teased her. He waved a pretzel in her face, and nearly dripped mustard down the front of her dress.

"Don't come near me, creep," Tracy said absently. She glanced around the room, trying to catch a glimpse of Joshua's blond hair.

"If you're looking for Nora and Jen, they went to Temptations. They said they'd meet you there." He paused, and stuck his hand out. "That will be fifty cents."

"Forget it," Tracy snapped. Where was Joshua? Then the crowd shifted and she spied him at the food table. Brushing Jason aside, she hurried to his side.

When he spotted her, his face lit up in a welcoming grin. "Hey, I wondered what happened to you. All the food's almost gone," he said, handing her a piece of pizza on a paper plate. Joshua had changed into a pair of jeans and a white sweater over an oxford-cloth shirt. We look wonderful together, Tracy thought happily.

"Who needs food?" she said breathlessly. She took the piece of pizza reluctantly, still smiling at him. Maybe if she ate it fast, they could leave. . . .

"Have to keep your energy up," Joshua

said seriously. "I know how you girls are. You probably didn't eat a bite before the play tonight."

"Well, actually — " Tracy began, but was interrupted by a short girl with curly red hair.

"That's right!" the redhead burst out. "I remember the first time I was in a play, I was too nervous to eat, and my stomach growled through the whole first act."

Tracy smiled politely, willing the girl to drop through the floor. Who was this pest, and what did she want? And why was she standing so close to Joshua?

At that moment, Joshua kiddingly hit himself in the head. "Gee, where are my manners? I forgot, you guys don't know each other."

That's okay, Tracy longed to say, I don't want to know this person! She dumped the piece of pizza on the table and took a step closer to Joshua. The sooner they got out of here, the better. She didn't like the way the redhead was smiling at him.

"Carol, this is Tracy Douglas, a really great actress."

"Nice to met you," Tracy said, smiling prettily.

"And Tracy, this is Carol Hillman, my girl friend."

Carol Hillman, my girl friend! Tracy felt her smile freeze on her face. It couldn't be true! Carol was saying something to her, but it might as well have been in Swahili, because none of it registered on Tracy's brain.

She did a quick inventory of Carol Hillman, girl friend. The girl was *plain*, no doubt about it, with freckly white skin — the kind that never tans, Tracy thought — and wild red hair that smothered her little face with curls.

"Well, it looks like it's time to split," Joshua was saying. Tracy forced herself to look at him. "We're on our way to another party over at St. Edmond's. That's where Carol goes to school," he explained.

"Of course," Tracy said, taking a giant gulp of her soft drink. She wanted to scream at both of them, she wanted to spill her drink all over Carol's blue T-shirt, she wanted to stamp her foot in frustration. Since none of these things were possible, she did the next best thing. She looked at her watch and said in mock horror, "Oh, my goodness, I'm late for a party myself." She plunked her drink on the table. "Got to run! Nice to meet you, Carol. So long, Joshua." And before either of them could say another word, she was moving quickly through the crowd, out of the room, out of the building, out of Joshua's life.

Meanwhile, Denise was wandering

around backstage, with a forced smile on her face. She was trying to look happy, but inside, her stomach was churning with anxiety. Where was Cody? She waved to a freshman in the chorus and began another slow circle of the wings. It's crazy, she thought irritably. I've checked the prop room, the dressing room, the makeup room . . . . Where could he have disappeared to?

She hadn't had time to remove her makeup, and she wondered if she dared risk a peek in the theater lobby. Mr. Morgan had strictly forbidden them to appear in costume, but this was an emergency.

She was hesitating offstage when she heard a low voice that made her heart stop. "Thanks for all your help, guys," Cody's deep voice rumbled from the lighting booth. Denise turned to see him heading for the side exit door.

"Cody!" she blurted out. He looked around, puzzled, and she hurried over to him. Something was wrong, very wrong . . . . He had already changed into a light blue shirt and khaki pants, and he was holding a set of car keys in his hands. . . .

"Hey," he said casually, raising a hand in greeting. He paused with his hand on the metal door. "What's up?"

"I . . . uh. . . ." Now that Denise had his attention, she couldn't think of a thing to say. "The party's downstairs," she said lightly.

Cody laughed. "The cast party?" He lowered his voice. "Sorry, that's not my style."

Denise flushed, and moved a little closer to him. She ducked as someone carried a plywood flat by them. "No, of course not," she said hurriedly. She waited for him to say something. He must have made other plans for them, she thought, relief washing over her. That was it, she thought giddily. They were going to have their own private celebration!

Cody shifted his weight and jangled his car keys. He seemed eager to leave, and Denise said brightly, "It will only take me a minute to change."

Cody's dark eyes look blank. "Change?" he repeated.

"For the next stop tonight," Denise said gaily. "Where are we going, anyway? Do you think Primavera's will be too crowded? I feel like eating a double order of lasagna!"

Cody frowned. "Well, actually. . . ." He ducked his head and ran his hand through his hair. He seemed to be staring at a point somewhere over her right ear, and Denise resisted the impulse to turn around.

Why does he look so uncomfortable? Denise wondered. Maybe he's tired. Maybe the last thing he wants is to be around other people. Impulsively, she moved closer, and looked up into his dark eyes.

"I've got a better idea," she said softly. "Why don't we go back to my house? We'll have a light pasta salad and play some records on the stereo."

"Denise," he said, in a hoarse voice. He moved slightly so her hands fell to her sides, and she stepped back, embarrassed. "Look, I don't know how to say this. . . ."

"Say what?" she asked, puzzled. "I won't be disappointed if we don't go anywhere, honest," she said earnestly. She smiled at him. "After all, the important thing is that we're together tonight."

He shook his head. "That's what I'm trying to tell you, Denise," he said, not meeting her eyes. "We can't see each other tonight."

She waited, frozen, while he shuffled his feet. "Why not?" she asked at last. Her heart was hammering, but she refused to let him see how upset she was.

"I've got . . . uh . . . other plans," he said, finally. There was a long silence, and somewhere in the background Denise heard shouts of laughter. The cast party must be in full swing. . . .

"In fact, I'm running a little late," he said apologetically. He glanced at his watch and took his sunglasses out of his pocket.

"Big party?" Denise said, forcing a bright smile on her face. She couldn't believe it! He was leaving her to go out with someone else!

Cody gave her the same thumbs-up gesture that Danny had used throughout the play. "Hey," he said, using Danny's accent, "what can I tell you?"

That line always got a laugh in the play, but Denise couldn't keep the smile on her face. "I thought . . . I thought we had something special going," she blurted out. She hated herself for saying it, but she couldn't let him go without a word, without knowing how she really felt about him.

"We did," Cody said casually, "but the play's over. It's been a lot of fun working with you, Denise." He grinned then, and for a moment, Denise thought she would burst into tears. How could she have been so wrong about him? She was *sure* he had cared about her!

"That's it?" she demanded. "That's all you're going to say — it's been . . . fun?"

Cody's dark eyes clouded, then he leaned down and kissed her very lightly on the lips. "C'mon, Denise," he said coaxingly. "We're not onstage now."

"I know we're not onstage," she said indignantly. "But I thought — "

"You're the best," he said absently, cutting her off. He carefully polished his sunglasses before putting them on. "See ya around." He seemed eager to leave, and Denise couldn't think of a single reason to make him stay. What was there left to say, anyway? He pushed open the stage door and stepped out into the night.

Denise raised her small hand and then let it drop to her side. "Yeah, see ya," she whispered. She felt tears brimming up in her eyes, and willed them not to spill down her cheeks. She quickly brushed her hand over her eyes, and when she looked up the doorway was empty.

Cody was gone.

"Here's to the Pink Ladies," Nora shouted, her chocolate frosted raised in a toast. It was a little after eleven, and she and her friends were crowded into a back booth at Temptations.

"Let's hear it for the chorus," Lucy Armanson said, holding her strawberry milk shake in the air. "The best singers and dancers in all of Cedar Groves." She smiled at Nora. "With one exception."

"Very funny," Nora said, trying to swat Lucy with a napkin. "At least I got through that flying leap tonight."

"And I managed to hit a high C in the second song," Jen said proudly. "All in all, I think we've got a lot to be grateful for."

Amy Williams noisily sipped her butterscotch delight and said to Jen, "Are you still going to make acting your career?"

Jen flushed and bit her lip. "Well, I've been kind of having second thoughts about that," she admitted.

"Really?" Nora looked surprised.

Jen nodded. "I like being onstage tonight," she went on. "But I'm not sure it's what I really want to do with my life."

"There was too much work and too many late nights for me," Lucy pointed out. "I'm still five chapters behind in everything." She giggled. "The rest of Mr. Robards' history class is studying Napoleon, and I never got past Charlemagne." She finished her drink and ordered another. "Hey, look who's outside!" She gestered to the front window where Tracy and Denise were standing on the sidewalk, deep in conversation. "I had almost given up on them."

Outside, Denise and Tracy looked at each other in surprise. "I never expected to see you here tonight," Tracy said hesitantly. "I thought you and Cody — "

"Would be out together?" Denise finished the sentence for her. "No," she said wryly. She thought back to the scene at the stage door. "I'm afraid Cody . . . had other plans. With someone else."

Tracy looked at her sympathetically. "Oh, wow," she said softly. "I'm sorry."

"It's okay," Denise said quickly. "Actually, it's *not* okay, but it will be, eventually." She paused. "What happened with you and that blond guy in the chorus . . . Jonathan?"

"Joshua," Tracy said. She sighed and then gave a wistful smile. "Like they say, he's history."

They stood looking at each other for a moment and then Denise chuckled. "Show business is sure full of surprises, isn't it?"

Tracy nodded. "Joshua was so terrific," she said wistfully. "He reminded me of someone I saw in a movie once. . . ."

"Actors can be dangerous," Denise said wryly. "They can make you see things that aren't there. I was positive that Cody was really interested in me . . . right up until the end."

"That's exactly the way I felt about Joshua!" Tracy stared at her, her blue eyes serious. "He was so nice to me all the time, and he persuaded me to stay in the play. I thought I really meant something to him."

"I know what you mean," Denise said sympathetically.

"And then tonight he turned up with this awful girl from St. Edmond's!" Tracy flinched at the memory of the freckled redhead. "He actually introduced her as his *girl friend*! I wanted to fall through the floor. Can you imagine how embarrassing it was?"

"I can imagine, because I was in the same boat. Cody was on his way to a party with another girl. It's no fun not being taken seriously," Denise said softly.

"Gee, I can't imagine anyone not taking you seriously, Denise. I thought you could always wrap boys around your finger."

"Not this one," Denise said thoughtfully. "He was older, you know." She shrugged. "Maybe that had something to do with it. I think part of the problem is that we don't have enough experience. Maybe someday we'll learn how to smell a rat a mile away."

"Even a block away would help," Tracy said, nodding her head so vigorously her blonde hair bounced up and down.

Denise laughed and pushed open the door to Temptations. "Oh, Tracy," she said, smiling, "promise me you'll never change!"

Arm in arm, they made their way to the back booth in Temptations. "Room for two more?" Tracy called out gaily.

"No, but we'll squeeze you in," Jen told her. "How come you're not at the cast party?" she asked, curious.

Denise and Tracy exchanged a look. "It's a long story," Denise explained. She looked around the crowded table. "I notice none of you stayed long, either," she said shrewdly.

"It was funny," Nora said, "but I didn't feel we really belonged there. With the high school kids, I mean."

Lucy nodded. "I know what you mean," she agreed. "Everyone got along really well during the play, but once it's over, we really didn't have much to say to each other. Didn't you feel that way, Mia?"

"I sure did," Mia said firmly. She had wiped off her pancake makeup but was still wearing heavy eyeliner and shadow. "I couldn't wait to get over here. Andy and the rest of the guys will be joining us soon."

"Well, you have to admit, it's been fun," Jen said after a minute. "A once-in-a-lifetime experience."

"That's true," Nora replied. "And I want to keep it that way. I want to have my life back!" She'd go into school early on Monday, she decided. Maybe her biology experiment hadn't turned to dust, and she could start working on it again.

"C'mon, it was all worthwhile," Amy put in.

"It sure was — we met some cute guys," Tracy said with a faraway look on her face. "One cute guy," she amended.

"One's all you need!" Mia hooted.

"Even if he didn't stick around long," Tracy said in a low voice.

"There will be plenty of other boys," Jen said kindly.

"But will they be gorgeous?" Tracy asked.

"You'll just have to wait and see." Mia looked mysterious. "Maybe they'll have other qualities that are more important."

"But I want them to be perfect!" Tracy wailed.

Lucy giggled. "Grow up, Tracy. You can't have your cake and eat it, too."

Suddenly a freckled arm reached out and snatched Lucy's fudge cake right out from under her nose. "Oh, yes, you can!" Jason yelled in her ear. "Just watch this." He took an enormous bite and then, holding the cake high above his head, whizzed down the aisle on his skateboard.

He didn't stop as he reached the glass doors at the front of the restaurant. Everyone waited for the crash. But then Andy Warwick and Mitch Pauley suddenly opened the doors, and Jason sailed right through, cackling wildly.

"What was all that about?" Andy asked when he reached the table.

Nora laughed and looked at Jen. "I think it means," she said softly, "that things are finally back to normal."

The kids in the eighth grade aren't ready for the wacky romance that develops when a gorgeous new French exchange student arrives! Read Junior High #9, WHO'S THE JUNIOR HIGH HUNK?